Danger on the Quarry Path

Meg Ashley

Regal Books

A Division of GL Publications
Ventura, California, U.S.A.

**Other books in the Boarding House Adventure
series by Meg Ashley:**
The Secret of the Old House
Lights in the Lake
Deserted Rooms

Rights for publishing this book in other languages are contracted by Gospel Litera-
ture International foundation (GLINT). GLINT also provides technical help for
the adaptation, translation, and publishing of Bible study resources and books in
more than 100 languages worldwide. For further information, contact GLINT,
Post Office Box 6688, Ventura, California 93006, U.S.A., or the publisher.

Scripture quotations in this publication are from the *New American Standard
Bible*. The Lockman Foundation 1960, 1962, 1963, 1968, 1971, 1972, 1973,
1975. Used by permission.

Published by Regal Books
A Division of GL Publications
Ventura, California 93006
Printed in U.S.A.

Library of Congress Cataloging in Publication Data.

Ashley, Meg, 1948—
    Danger on the quarry path.

    (Boarding house adventure ; #4)
    Summary: Beth and Joey become involved in Middle Eastern politics when a
train crash brings the crown prince of Shamir to the boarding house.
    [1. Mystery and detective stories]   I. Title.
II. Series: Boarding house adventure ; 4.
PZ7.A82643Dan   1985   [Fic]   85-1966
ISBN 0-8307-1034-5

To Bob
for being there.

Chapter 1

Beth's feet hurt. She glanced down at her new high-heeled shoes and tried to wiggle her toes. *The price of beauty is high,* she thought.

The 14-year-old girl was in the lavender bedroom on the second floor of the house. She looked in the full-length mirror attached to the closet door and surveyed herself carefully.

Not bad, she decided. Her red hair had gained a burnished glow in the last year, her freckles had faded and, if she sucked in her stomach, she even had something close to a figure.

Another person moved into the mirror's reflection. "My turn," Beth's mother said. The slender dark-haired woman carefully placed an ivory colored veiled hat on her head and pulled the short netting down over her eyes. "It's almost time."

Beth could hear the hum of voices coming up from downstairs. She'd made several trips that Friday afternoon to the bedroom across the hall to watch people arrive at the boarding house. She wondered now how there could possibly be room for everyone in the parlor.

Soft strains of piano music mixed with the sounds of concurrent conversations. Beth picked up the long-stemmed rose she would carry and toyed with the blossom.

"Joey's getting pretty good, huh, Mom?"

Virginia nodded through the mirror. "If he doesn't break his fingers playing ball. I thought I'd have to get another pianist after your last game."

A knock sounded at the door and an elderly lady peeked into the room. "Ready, girls?"

Beth stood beside her mother at the mirror. "Everything's going to be different now, isn't it?"

Virginia saw the expression on Beth's face and pulled her close. "It'll be different, but it'll be better."

Strains of the wedding march began and Beth resolutely left the room and walked to the top of the stairs. Memories raced through her mind as she slowly descended the carpeted steps: memories of her childhood in Los Angeles; of finding out she was adopted, yet knowing that Ed and Virginia Cooper were Dad and Mom; then her dad's cancer and death. She remembered the sad years after that when her mom seemed to be dead inside, then the day the lawyer called with advice to sell Grandpa Cooper's farm in northern Idaho, a two-hundred-acre parcel of land that was theirs by inheritance.

They'd come north to see the land before selling it, and in spite of the prevailing state of neglect, they'd seen something very beautiful in the old house. Underneath the dust and disrepair, the house had seemed alive and wanting to be lived in again.

They had decided to stay. Virginia hired Chuck Warren, a local carpenter and the pastor of the small church in Cooper's Creek, to handle the renovation. Now, every room of the house was restored. Every bedroom was done in a different color scheme, and had a different feel. The people who came as boarders always found a room suited to them. The wooden banisters and hardwood floors gleamed; the carved moldings around the ceilings of the main rooms downstairs had been repaired, the walls re-papered, even the brick and marble fireplaces—all four of them—looked as they had when they were first built.

It had been an expensive project and one that forced Virginia to open the house to boarders. Even that income had not been enough, and last summer, if they hadn't discovered an artesian well on their land, they might have had to move. The sale of that sweet water gave them enough money to relax.

And now this, Beth thought as she stepped off the last step and faced the roomful of people in the parlor.

Sheriff Larsen stood in front of the fireplace beside Chuck, who was now functioning as a pastor. The lawman was out of uniform of course, and for the first time since Beth had met him, he looked nervous.

Joey Daggett, Beth's best friend, caught her eye

and grinned at her over the piano where he sat playing. Ever since Joey was left without parents, he had lived with Chuck Warren. The young pastor not only filled the role of legal guardian, but also supplied the life-scarred Joey with a home and hope of healing. The 16-year-old looked unusually handsome in his gray suit. This was the first time in months Beth had seen him without his blonde hair sticking out from under a baseball cap. She hoped he appreciated the hours she'd spent choosing a dress and fixing her hair.

Virginia entered the room behind her daughter and once she stood beside the sheriff, the wedding began. The ceremony didn't last long and Beth wondered at how quickly such a change in her life could be transacted. After the photographer was finished and the cake cut, she slipped away from the crowd.

She kicked off her shoes and stared out the parlor window. A wind had risen and was whipping the bare-limbed trees in the front yard. The winter had been mild; now as spring took hold, the weather seemed determined to get even. One storm after another swept across the Canadian border.

"I hope we don't get rained out Sunday," a familiar voice said from behind her. "And I hope you're not too lame to play."

Beth looked at her swollen feet, then noticed that Joey had stripped off his tie and loosened his collar.

"We've got to win," he added.

Beth sighed and turned back to watch the clouds moving across the sky.

"You'll get to play," Joey consoled her. "If you

keep your eye on the ball, you can probably get a hit off Tommy Jenkins. He's not such a hot pitcher."

Beth didn't respond.

Joey punched her playfully on the shoulder. "Cheer up, Red. Your mom's not dying. She's just getting married."

The girl walked outside and stood on the front porch, leaning on the railing. The wind played with her skirt and pulled at her curls.

"Why do things have to change?" she asked when she heard Joey come up behind her. "Everything is changing. Mom, me, us," she looked up at Joey and saw the deepness time had hidden in his young eyes. "Even the weather. The newsman said there's never been a year like this for crazy weather." She shivered. "I don't like it. Sometimes I feel like the whole world is going crazy. It's scary."

Joey couldn't answer right away. He used his tie to practice tying square knots. "Remember that guy Chuck talked about in church a while back? Maybe it was Joshua. I forget. Anyway, he was the one who asked God to hold the sun still in the sky so the Israelites could finish fighting."

Beth couldn't follow his line of thought. She looked at him quizzically. "Yeah, I guess."

"Well, God did what he asked. God used his prayers to change things, to change history. There's lots of things like that in the Bible."

"So what's that got to do with anything?" Beth asked.

Joey sighed. "Maybe the world *is* going crazy, but I think what God wants us to know is that one man, one person can make a difference. One person can change history."

Beth turned back to face the yard. "Yeah, well, I wish somebody'd show up quick."

A fierce gust of wind swept across the yard. The tree branches were lifted and the bare limbs wrestled with the wind.

A gust of cold air hit the porch and hurled its icy blast against the house. Beth turned her back against the onslaught and Joey shielded her against himself. There was more to the coldness than just the March wind blowing into April. "Winter is over, Beth," he whispered. "It always gives up eventually."

Beth and Joey were playing catch in the shelter of the backyard when Paul and Virginia walked outside with their luggage. Beth was watching them when Joey burned the ball across the width of the yard. Luckily, she heard it coming.

"Catch it or die!" Joey yelled.

The padding in Beth's glove was less than adequate and she yelped when she caught it.

"I'm on *your* team!" she protested. She tucked her hand under her arm and walked to the sheriff's car where her new stepfather was loading the trunk.

"Two weeks isn't such a long time," Virginia said when she saw Beth's glum expression.

Beth looked at her mother as though she were a stranger. "Nothing will be the same when you get back," she stated simply.

"Maybe you'll have done most of the changing," Virginia suggested. "I love you, Beth. That won't change. And real love can put up with any kind of change and be stronger for it. Don't worry. Love is stronger than any other force in the world."

Paul approached them and stood aside while Beth kissed her mother good-bye. He didn't expect the embrace that Beth gave him.

"Take care of the house," he said after the hug. "We've got a lot of happy memories to make in there."

A train's whistle in the distance lent a lonely note to the farewells. The sky was overcast and the wind continued to blow in cold, capricious gusts. Beth watched the car until it drove out of sight.

The passenger train that cut through the forest 15 miles to the north had a bullet's dullness under the darkening skies. As night came, only the lights in the cars hinted of warmth or life. The last two passenger cars were different from the others. One was a sleeping coach with spacious private rooms. The other was a lounge, with plush seating, small tables and a private bar. Five men sat within; three with bulges under their coats played at a game of dice at one end of the car.

The fourth man was older than the others, gray-haired and had something of a regal air about him. His dark brown face was sharply featured and his eyes moved like a hawk's, seeing everything, yet remaining inscrutable to anyone who tried to read them. He wore a thick gold ring on each hand and around his neck a heavy chain that carried a thick gold medallion. His long fingers often touched the token as though it were charmed.

The fifth person in the car was the youngest. At moments he looked to be in his twenties. Any youthfulness of his true 17 years had vanished long ago. His face was smooth but tense, his eyes clear but wary. He wore a turban and a western-style suit tailored by the finest house in London. His face was unblemished and fine, handsome, but sad.

"Ahmed," the elderly statesman spoke. His voice was soft, yet piercing. Even the guards at their table in the back stopped to see if they were being summoned. "You see how it goes," he went on. "The American people are foolish like children. Their wealth and power has numbed them to the realities of life. They think the way they live is their right even though the world starves. Their power justifies everything they do."

"But they are a good people, Jorge," the young man countered. "Else my father would not have sent me here. He wants them for our allies."

"Your father . . . " Jorge began.

"My father rules our land," Ahmed cut in sharply.

Jorge turned away, but as he looked at his own reflection in the dark window, he smiled.

A steward in a crisp white jacket served dinner to the envoy in their private lounge car. The man was serving coffee when the train lurched. Ahmed and Jorge were nearly thrown from their chairs and the steward fell to the floor amid a crash of breaking china.

The guards jumped to their feet and pulled the guns free from their shoulder holsters. The train lurched again and this time everyone was thrown to the floor. The lights in the cars went out. Screams from people in the forward cars were drowned out by a tremendous crash.

Ahmed felt himself being lifted into the air and thrown like a limp doll against the side of the car.

The car seemed suspended in space, and then tables and chairs mixed with bodies as the car was hurled from the rails and tumbled down the mountainous embankment.

Ahmed tried to scream but in his mind came only one word, "Allah." Then pain enveloped him until all was dark and quiet.

Word of the train crash spread quickly across the Idaho countryside. The telephone at the boarding house rang, issuing a summons to Sheriff Larsen.

"He's not here," Chuck answered. "He's on his honeymoon. What's wrong?"

Beth and Joey were sitting at the dining room table eating popcorn. They stopped spitting kernels at each other long enough to listen.

"Where?" Chuck asked. "Okay, I'll leave now."

He slammed down the receiver, grabbed his jacket and hurried to the back door.

"I'm coming," Joey declared. "I can help."

Chuck barred his way at the door. "It's bad, Joey, real bad. The express from Portland derailed at the Manhacket bridge. There's not going to be many survivors. That gorge is steep."

Joey slipped into his windbreaker. "You're going to need help," he said quietly. "Those people are going to need help, as much as they can get."

Chuck weighed the boy's words and searched for something in his eyes. "Okay," he said. "Come on."

Beth followed them to the truck. "How about me?"

"No way!" Chuck snapped. "But I'll tell you what. There may be some people who need a place to stay for a few days. You can get some beds made up. We might be bringing home a few boarders."

"I'm always stuck in right field," Beth grumbled as she kicked a rock back to the house.

Chuck and Joey had to take logging roads to get to the scene of the accident. Other vehicles were already there; ambulances and sheriff's cars were streaming to the sight. A helicopter hovered overhead and held a huge spotlight on the scene. Men had fastened hooks to the trestle of the bridge and were lowering lightweight metal stretchers down the sides of the gorge to bring up the injured.

Joey blanched and staggered when he saw the dead. Chuck felt him falter and steadied him. "You okay?"

Joey swallowed the bile that had risen in his throat and took a deep breath. "Yeah."

"The dead are God's," Chuck said. "Concentrate on the living."

The bodies of the three guards were taken away early in the rescue operation. Ahmed was found thrown free of the wreckage and was carefully brought to the top of the gorge. A paramedic checked him over as he hurried from one victim to another. Joey saw the youth and watched the medic's ministrations.

"He's okay," the man declared. "Shaken up pretty bad, maybe some head injuries. I don't know. He's in shock, but he got off lucky."

Other injured people were being laid beside the tracks.

"Find him a blanket or something," the medic ordered as he hurried away. "Keep him warm."

Joey ran to the truck and found the blanket

Chuck kept behind the seat. He covered Ahmed and carefully tucked the blanket around his body. The wind was dying down, but the night was cold.

"Jorge?" Ahmed murmured. "Jorge?"

"It's okay," Joey assured him. "You're okay."

Ahmed's eyes opened and slowly focused. He first saw the stars glittering like crystal between the scudding clouds. Then he saw the face of a stranger, a boy, hovering over him. He tried to sit up, but fell back weakly. "Where is Jorge?"

"They're still finding people," Joey told him. "Is he your father?"

"No . . . my advisor . . . I . . . " and then he reverted to his own language and Joey sensed the words were a prayer. He laid a hand on Ahmed's shoulder and left to find Chuck.

The rescue operation was nearly over by the time Joey located his guardian. Chuck was helping the paramedics load the badly injured into the waiting ambulances. The helicopter pulled away as the last ambulance turned around and drove slowly down the fire-break to the logging road. Chuck squatted on his heels and stared at the gorge. He looked at his foster son as Joey approached.

"Bad, bad business," the young pastor said. "Two dozen dead and three times that many injured."

"What happened?" Joey asked.

"The rain washed out part of the cliff. When the train's weight hit the bridge, the trestles gave way. No support. We haven't found the engineer. He went to the bottom with the engine."

"There's a guy, over there," Joey pointed. "Some kind of foreigner. I think you ought to talk to him."

Sheriff's deputies were questioning passengers who had escaped injury and vans were taking many of them off the site. Chuck let Joey lead him to where Ahmed was sitting beside the tracks.

The young prince looked up as they approached. "They needed the stretchers. I guess I'm not hurt badly. Did you find my men?"

Chuck sat on the rail. "It's going to take some time to sort out who's dead and who's injured. It'll be a while before everyone is identified. Right now we're most concerned with getting medical attention for everyone. Are you a visitor to this country?"

Ahmed nodded. "My name is Ahmed Gabreel."

Chuck pulled away. "Gabreel? Of Shamir? Are you . . . ? I read about your trip, but, excuse me, you can't stay here. Joey, help me get him to the truck." Then to Ahmed, "If you will allow us, I'll take you to the home of a friend. It's a simple home, but gracious. Please, for tonight at least." He helped Ahmed to his feet and Joey wondered at the deference Chuck gave the young man.

"Tomorrow," Chuck went on, "we'll contact the authorities. I'm sure my country's State Department will supply you with an escort."

Ahmed nodded his consent and did not speak again on the trip to the boarding house. Once they arrived, Chuck helped the young man upstairs.

"What're you giving him the green room for?" Beth protested. "It's the biggest one! The red room's ready too."

Chuck silenced her with a glance.

"What's the big deal with him?" Beth whispered to Joey. "Some guy called just before you got here and said they needed a bunch of people to stay here a while. We're gonna need that room!"

Joey raised his eyebrows. "He's some kind of hotshot from overseas," he explained.

Chuck came up behind them. "He's the crown prince, I guess you'd call it, of Shamir," he filled in. "Our government is negotiating a trade agreement with his country right now. With his father, as a matter of fact."

"Ouch!" Beth murmured. "Royalty?"

"In a manner of speaking," Chuck nodded.

An hour later, Beth tiptoed upstairs carrying her mother's silver platter. She'd taken a cup from the best set of china and made some instant cocoa. She balanced the platter carefully on one arm as she knocked softly on Ahmed's bedroom door.

"Your highness?" she called softly.

"Yes," permission came.

Beth had a hard time getting the door open without losing the tray. "I thought you might like a little something to help you sleep." She set the platter on the dresser. "It's just hot cocoa, but my mom gives it to me when I can't sleep. Works every time."

Ahmed was sitting on the bed, propped up against the headboard. He'd lost his turban in the crash and now his jet black hair was carefully combed. Beth would have curtsied if she'd known how. He watched her carry the cup to him. She was shaking so hard the cocoa slopped into the saucer.

"You are very kind," Ahmed said as he took it from her.

"Thank you, Your Highness." Beth backed away respectfully.

"This is your house?" Ahmed asked.

"Yeah, I mean yes. My great-great-grandfather built it when they drove the Indians off the land. He was one of the first settlers."

"Quaint," Ahmed observed.

"I like it 'cause it's so big!" Beth said.

Ahmed smiled slightly.

"I'll bet you have a big house," Beth stated, trying to do something with her hands. Finally she put them behind her back.

"Considerably bigger than this," he replied as he held out the empty cup for her to take. "We have a palace in the capital and three others in the country."

"Oh," Beth gulped. "Do you ride camels?"

Ahmed's smile was one of toleration. "I have, but mostly I drive a Mercedes."

"Your dad lets you drive his car?" Beth asked.

"No, *my* car. I have others, but I prefer the German model."

Beth's eyes widened. "Your family must be loaded!"

Ahmed seemed offended. "We have oil in my country," he stated simply.

Joey appeared at the open door. His face tightened when he saw Beth standing at the foot of the bed. "Chuck wants you," he told her. "People are here from the train."

"You should hear about this, Joey," the girl said as she left the room. "I bet he even has servants!"

Joey stood in the doorway and looked the young man over carefully. "You play any ball?" he asked. "Or are you too busy counting your money?"

"Ball?" Ahmed asked, ignoring the insult. "Play ball? No," he replied. "I don't have time to play."

Joey shrugged. "Yeah, well, tough life," he said. "By the way," he added as he started to close the door. "Breakfast is at 7:30. You'll have to come downstairs. We don't serve breakfast in bed. To anyone."

———————————

At the hospital in Coeur d'Alene, two men from the train were treated for minor injuries and released. They stood at the nurses' station and the shorter of the two leaned over the counter to talk to the young nurse on duty.

"I could really use a good meal," he said. "You probably know of some nice restaurant around here, don't you? A pretty girl like you must have plenty of dates."

The nurse blushed. "Mr. Martin, the cafeteria is where I eat. It's in the west wing."

"West wing? Can you show me?"

She came out of the nursing station and guided him to an intersection of halls a hundred feet away. As soon as her back was turned, the other, older man quickly looked through the patients' charts. He found the one he wanted, noted the room number at the top, then nodded to his partner.

"Shall we, Mr. Randolph?" the younger man called back down the hall. "Thanks," he said to the nurse and the two men quickly walked away.

"He's here, the old buzzard," Randolph said quietly. "The boy's not listed."

"Maybe he's dead."

Randolph shook his head. "We couldn't be so lucky. This job isn't going to be that easy."

They stood outside the hospital talking quietly then separated and went in opposite directions, disappearing into the wind-whipped streets of Coeur d'Alene.

Chapter 2

Chuck woke Beth early the next morning. "You've got to help me with breakfast," he explained. "We've got a lot of people to feed."

Beth had all four of her mother's skillets on the stove and was cooking pancakes when the first guests started coming downstairs. A family on their way to a new home in Pocatello sat down at the table. There were three little girls in the Trevor family, all under the age of five. One was an infant who cried fretfully despite the young mother's efforts to comfort her.

Beth crossed her eyes and clenched her teeth as the crying grated on her nerves.

"Just keep cooking," Chuck murmured as he pulled a tray of bacon from the oven.

Soon the table was surrounded. An older couple from Canada was still shaken from their experience on the train and hardly ate. When Eva and May, the two older Trevor girls, started eating pancakes with their fingers, the Canadian couple took their coffee to the parlor.

Mrs. Hazelton, a heavy-set woman in a flowing Hawaiian dress, was oblivious to the confusion and sat at the table chattering excitedly about her adventure.

By the time Ahmed descended the stairs to the dining room, Beth's forehead was beaded with perspiration. He paused at the bottom of the stairs as though he expected everyone to rise to their feet.

"How do you like your eggs?" Beth shouted over the table talk. "Scrambled is safest."

Chuck wiped his hands on a towel and offered Ahmed a clean spot at the table, away from Eva and May.

Ahmed nodded his thanks. "Coffee first," he said. "Then perhaps some fruit."

Beth brought another platter of pancakes to the table and forked two onto Ahmed's empty plate. "These are pretty good. I think I'm getting them cooked all the way through now. You have to watch the bubbles, you know."

Ahmed looked at the strange food with some misgivings. He cut into them and grimaced as he chewed.

"Don't you want some syrup?" Beth asked. "They don't taste like much plain."

"I think I've had enough," he said and motioned for Beth to take the plate away.

The young father, John Trevor, was trying to

feed May and keep Eva from standing up on her chair when Joey walked in the front door. A big wolf-dog wearing a black patch over one eye, trotted in beside him. Mrs. Hazelton gasped and nearly choked on her mouthful of food.

John Trevor jumped to his feet, knocking over his chair. "Is that critter safe? I shoot varmints like that back home!"

The wolf-dog stopped and quietly bared his fangs.

"Put Furball outside," Chuck ordered Joey. "For now," he added when he saw the look on the boy's face.

Joey was dressed in ragged blue jeans and a sweaty T-shirt. He looked like he'd already put in a full day's labor.

"How'd it go?" Chuck asked when Joey took a seat at the table. Beth set a plateful of pancakes in front of him and sat down beside him.

"Okay," the boy mumbled. "I've only got one weekend left."

"What kind of labor do you perform?" Ahmed asked as he carefully ate the fresh fruit compote Chuck had fixed especially for him.

"County work," Joey answered crisply.

"Public service," Beth added. "That's his sentence."

"Sentence?" Ahmed looked at the boy carefully. "You are a convict?"

Joey glared at Beth, then turned on Ahmed. "Yeah, I guess you could put it that way. I dig ditches every Saturday morning and wear a ball and chain." He returned to his eating and inhaled his food, hardly stopping to breathe. When his plate was empty, he stomped out of the room. "I'm going swimming," he called back to Chuck. "The stream has cleaned out the pool real well."

Ahmed raised his eyebrows. "I take it he is a delinquent."

Chuck's face tightened. "He's my foster son. He made a bad decision, used some bad judgment once, and now he's paying for it. That doesn't make him bad, just human. No one is immune from making mistakes."

Ahmed didn't look convinced.

"He's a really hot pitcher," Beth inserted as she removed Ahmed's dirty dishes. "Maybe you ought to come to our next ballgame. Joey's great!"

"I'm afraid I have some business to attend to," Ahmed responded. Then to Chuck he said, "You will please drive me to the hospital where the injured were taken. I must locate my men and salvage what I can of this journey."

Chuck looked at the disaster area in the kitchen and silenced his initial response to the order. "Of course," he answered, "whenever you're ready."

Beth took the pile of dirty dishes Chuck held and set them in the sink. "I can swim later," she said quietly. "Water's probably cold as ice anyway."

Martin was sitting in a car outside the hospital when a call came over his radio.

"The boy is alive," the voice said. "He's staying in a private home ten miles out of Cooper's Creek. The guards are dead."

"You think they'll scrap their operation?" Martin asked, his face gray with fatigue.

"Find out," the order came. "Keep tabs on Jorge. He's the kingpin."

Just then Chuck's pick-up truck pulled up outside the hospital and Ahmed and Chuck got out.

"The kid's here," Martin said and ended the communication.

The man lit a cigarette and patiently smoked it as he watched Ahmed disappear into the building. Then he straightened his tie, checked his appearance in the rear view mirror and stepped out of the car.

He found room 278 without any trouble and walked purposefully but slowly past it. He was very aware of the conversation going on inside. He understood most of the words; he'd been carefully trained to recognize the Arabic dialect.

Chuck, however, could not follow the conversation. It flowed quickly between the dark-skinned foreigners. All Chuck could glean from the exchange was the obvious concern from Ahmed and an air of urgency from Jorge.

"You must get me out of here," Jorge demanded. "I do not wish to remain under American care."

"I will call my father," Ahmed stated. "We will secure a flight home as soon as possible."

"No!" Jorge snapped, then sagged back against his pillow. "You do not understand," he added apologetically. He motioned to his bedside stand. "Get the papers in the drawer."

Ahmed obeyed and handed a folded sheet of paper and a small but weighted manila envelope to his advisor.

Jorge looked at Chuck. "Tell this man to leave us," he ordered the young man.

Ahmed turned politely to his host. "We have much to discuss," he explained in English. "Would you please wait for me in the lobby?"

Chuck nodded and left the room. His unexpected departure startled the man leaning against the wall outside the door. Martin turned away quickly.

Inside the room, Jorge, his hands shaking, opened the paper and spread it on the bedcovers. It was a map of Idaho with cities and towns clearly marked.

Then Jorge tore open the envelope and a small metal Star of David fell out.

"Jorge, what is this?" Ahmed gasped. "The Israelis? . . . "

"I cannot explain it all now," Jorge broke in. "It is really only a reminder. You must trust me. Place the star on the map."

Ahmed obeyed.

"This bottom corner point," Jorge pointed, "must lie on Coeur d'Alene, where we are now. This is our first stop."

"But you are in no condition to continue."

Jorge closed his eyes and fingered his medallion. "Our purpose in coming to America is more than you were told," he explained gravely. "Your father needed our help for a very delicate and important business transaction."

"Why wasn't I told?" Ahmed demanded. "I am his . . . "

Jorge raised his hand to silence him. "I know. You are your father's heir. He has good reasons for protecting you."

He looked the young man directly in the eyes. "There is treachery in our government, men who would sell out the highest goals of our people, who would demean us with unholy treaties. There is evil very close to your father. He is suspicious and very careful."

Ahmed reached for the telephone on the bedside stand.

Jorge hit his hand away. "Don't be a fool!" he barked. "Did you not hear me? There is no way you can talk freely with your father or he with you."

"But . . . "

Jorge closed his eyes again and took several slow, deep breaths. "You must have me released. Today. Take me to this house you spoke of. Our men are dead, but we can still accomplish much." He opened his eyes and the fierceness Ahmed saw there startled him. "We *must* continue."

Jorge folded up the paper and handed it and the metal star to Ahmed. "We will go. Now. I will explain the rest when we are in that house. I feel the walls here have ears."

———

Martin was reading a newspaper in the lobby when Chuck left with Ahmed and Jorge. The elderly statesman was taken to the waiting limousine in a wheelchair and looked very weak. Chuck followed in the pick-up and did not notice the car that stayed far behind them until they entered Cooper's Creek. Then there were no other cars on the road to camouflage his intent and Martin let the forward vehicles pull out of sight.

Chuck followed the limousine to the boarding house. By the time he parked the truck, he could no longer bridle his concern. "I would like to call our State Department," he said as he helped Jorge out of the car. "If your advisor hadn't threatened to make an international incident, the hospital would never have agreed to release him. He must have a nurse, at least, and you can't move around the country without an escort."

"It is not your decision to make," Ahmed replied as he helped Jorge to the house. And Chuck sensed his advice was not to be given until asked for.

In the old kitchen was a large assortment of luggage. The largest piece was a black steamer trunk.

"Our cases are here," Jorge noted in his native tongue. "That is good." His breathing was labored and he steadied himself on Ahmed's arm.

"Have our things brought to our rooms," Ahmed directed Joey, who was openly inspecting the new arrival.

"Who does he think he is?" Joey muttered to Chuck when he came inside.

"He *knows* who he is," Chuck replied as he hurried to help Ahmed.

Beth met Ahmed in the parlor. "Can't you guys share a room?" she asked. "You've got the biggest bedroom in the house. "'Sides, we might need the others."

When Beth saw the look on Chuck's face, she shook her head. "Well, maybe not. I'll get the blue room ready. It's right next door. Mr. and Mrs. Babcock left after their stuff got here," she told Chuck.

After Jorge was comfortably settled in his room, Ahmed escorted Beth and Chuck out of the room and firmly closed the door behind them.

"The man is right," Ahmed said, noting Jorge's pallor. "You must have a nurse and I must let my father know we are alive."

Jorge waved Ahmed closer. His voice was hardly more than a whisper. "I have contacted Professor Omar at the university. He will get news to your father. Now, get the papers—the star."

Ahmed was shaken by the man's weakness. "I am calling for a doctor. The American doctors are as good as ours."

"No!" Jorge ordered with effort. "There is little time. I had to know if the trunk . . . I did not want to die in the American hospital." He grasped the medallion and sagged weakly against his pillow. "You will bury me at the oasis of Kharuz."

Ahmed's face was pale. "You should have stayed in the hosp . . . "

Jorge's eyes flashed. "There is no time! Do you not understand? Open the map."

"I'm calling Father!" Ahmed cried and turned decisively for the door.

"If you do, you will only endanger him and yourself," Jorge said with anger. "Omar is the only man you can trust now."

"I trust my father."

"You must *protect* your father and *help* him," Jorge explained. "Our purpose in coming to America is vitally important. Omar must come now and finish for me. Call him. Tell him to come, now. It will only take a few days. And in the meantime, you must keep us on schedule."

He pulled the map close and with shaking hands lifted the star. He struggled to position the points on the paper. Pain in his chest made him groan. He grabbed Ahmed's arm. "Packages, at each point. Get them and g . . . and . . . " he gasped for breath. "Give them to Omar when he comes. Trust them only to Omar."

The metal star fell to the hardwood floor with a clang. Ahmed did not notice.

Beth and Joey were struggling with the luggage when they heard a high-pitched cry coming from Jorge's room. It sounded like an eagle's scream before it plummets to earth.

Somehow in the ensuing mayhem, lunch was served. Beth was hostess at the table, while Chuck went to Ahmed's side and stayed there, helping him make the decisions he had to make as a result of Jorge's death. Ahmed aged in the next few hours as officials were called, the body removed and arrangements made for its transport back to Shamir.

Later, Ahmed made one telephone call. "Professor Omar, please," he asked the overseas operator. "At the State University in Cahmil."

Half an hour later, when the call came through, Ahmed refused to take it. He stayed in his room.

When Beth finished her chores, she put on her bathing suit and went upstairs, wondering if she should invite Ahmed to join her for a swim. When she tiptoed to his bedroom door, she heard a strange, quiet chant coming from the room. She did not knock on the door; she kept on moving down the hall to the back stairs and ran for the stable.

The afternoon sun was warm as she rode her mare, Nutmeg, down the lane to the place where the artesian well had filled the quarry bottom to form a natural pool. Last fall, Virginia had had concrete poured to form a lip around the pool and had a diving board and benches installed. Joey was already there. His horse was tied in the shade and Furball was in the water with his master. The two were playing a game that looked a little rough, considering the wolf-dog's sharp teeth.

———————

Ahmed left the house late in the afternoon. He wore his native robes and carried only the map and star with him. He walked aimlessly down the lane, and was unaware of the trees and the gentle spring breeze that blew against his face. When he heard Beth's laughter coming through the trees, he headed for the quarry.

"Come on in!" Beth hollered, when she saw him petting the horses. Her next words were only a gargle as Joey pulled her under the water.

"Nice horses," Ahmed remarked to Joey as he squatted near the edge of the pool. "We have a stable of Arabians at home. I enjoy riding."

Joey pushed off backwards from the side of the pool. "Is there anything you don't have?" he asked caustically.

Beth tried to dunk Joey and ended up losing the struggle. When she came up sputtering, she decided she needed a reinforcement. "Come on in," she urged. "There's extra suits in the bathhouse. The water's really nice."

Ahmed hesitated only a moment before going to the bathhouse to change.

When he disappeared in the small changing room, Beth turned angrily on Joey. She swam out to where he was floating. "You're a jerk," she huffed, working frantically to tread water. "Golly, he just had all his friends die. He *is* a prince and he has a lot of things on his mind. You're just jealous and you're being a super-cruddy jerk!"

"He acts like he owns the whole world," Joey snapped.

"I'll bet he owns a lot more of it than you ever

will," Beth snapped back. "And," her head went under and she came up trying to float on her back, "I think he could use some friends right now."

"I'll bet he couldn't play ball if his life depended on it!" Joey scoffed. "He's so wonderful, he's probably never even gotten his lily-white hands dirty."

"He's a prince!" Beth exploded. "Why should he go crazy over a dumb game where a bunch of loonies knock a ball of string around?"

"You sure scream at the games!" Joey retorted. "I thought you were going to kill Tubs Malone when he nailed me at second last game."

Beth tried treading water again. "He was blocking the baseline! The big blub! And then he stepped on you!"

"See what I mean?" Joey laughed.

"What?"

"Maybe getting excited about a ball game isn't so dumb. *You* do it, every game."

Beth had to think as fast as she was paddling. "It's different for people like Ahmed," she decided.

"That's just my point," Joey said. "Maybe that's part of what's wrong with the world."

When Ahmed stepped out of the bathhouse, Beth went under for the third time. His body was sleek and brown, firmly honed and hinting of strength.

Beth surfaced, gasping for breath, caught sight of Ahmed diving into the pool, and sank again. She finally made it to the side of the pool and hung on. She was afraid to look at Ahmed again for fear she'd drown.

"You want to race me for a few laps," Joey yelled when Ahmed surfaced.

Ahmed took the challenge. "Yes, if you'd like."

By the tenth lap, Joey's arms felt like lead, but he wouldn't quit. Ahmed swam like a well-oiled machine; his breathing was steady and strong.

At the fifteenth lap, Joey's stroke faltered. "I think that's enough for now," he said, trying not to gasp for breath.

Ahmed smiled, swam to the edge of the pool and pulled himself out. Joey noticed that Ahmed was not even breathing hard.

Beth had been watching the exhibition from her perch on the end of the diving board. She looked at Joey and only just managed to keep her laughter in check.

Joey grabbed his towel, walked to where the horses were tied and led King away. He disappeared down the narrow quarry path.

"Your friend does not like to compete," Ahmed observed as he walked over to the girl.

"He doesn't like to lose," Beth corrected. She walked off the diving board and sat on the edge of the pool, dangling her feet in the water. She wished she'd put polish on her toenails.

"I wish you two could be friends," she said shyly. "You're both neat guys."

Ahmed hung a towel around his neck and sat down beside her. "Friends?" He laid back on the cement lip that ran around the edge of the pool and watched the breeze playing through the trees. "People like me do not have friends. It is not wise."

Beth noted the sadness in his voice and dipped her hand in the water before answering. "I'm sorry about the old man. It must be awful being stranded here by yourself."

Ahmed remained silent a moment. "It has always been lonely," he whispered. "I can trust no one. You never know whose hand holds a knife. But you can be certain that the dagger's thrust will come from someone close enough to make it a killing blow." He raised up on his elbows.

"That man, who just died, *he* was your friend, wasn't he?"

"Jorge?" Ahmed looked away. "He was my teacher, an advisor of sorts. He had a position very close to my father." Ahmed's thoughts took him far away and Beth waited before speaking again.

"Are you going home soon?"

Her question must have penetrated the distance; Ahmed came back to the present with a jolt. "I don't know," he admitted. "I'd like to, but Jorge . . . " Ahmed shook his head. "But surely you do not want to hear the problems of state. I was told that American girls do not enjoy talking of serious matters."

Beth blushed. "I don't know about that. But I wouldn't be a bad friend. I don't even know how to use a knife."

Ahmed's tired face broke into a slight smile. He looked at her carefully, as though weighing something in his mind. Then he went to the bathhouse and returned, dressed in his robes and carrying the map and star. He spread the map on the cement and placed the star with one point lying on Coeur d'Alene. "Jorge was supposed to receive packages at each point. He asked me to stay and collect them for him. A man will come from my country and will take care of them." He lowered his eyes, obviously troubled.

"What's in them?" Beth asked as she rotated the star around the map.

"I don't know."

"Well, who's this man who's coming?"

"That's the problem," Ahmed admitted. "Professor Omar is a very influential man in my country, an intellectual."

"So, what's the problem with that? Does he know what's in the packages?"

"Probably." Ahmed's eyes met hers. He took a deep breath. "But I don't like the man. My father told me one time—it was late in the night and we had had riots at the university, protesting my father's intentions of establishing peaceful trade with America. My father was deeply troubled and," Ahmed stopped, then rushed to finish, "he cursed Omar."

Beth picked up the star and turned it over in her hand. "Call your dad," she offered. "Wouldn't that solve everything?"

Ahmed shook his head. "Jorge was adamant. I would endanger him terribly. Whatever this trip to America is, it is very delicate and very important. I must go ahead, alone."

Beth looked closely at Ahmed's worried face. "You really trusted this Jorge guy, didn't you?"

Ahmed nodded sadly. "Yes, second only to my father."

"Okay, then," Beth decided. She tossed the star down and stood up. "Let's get these dumb packages and call this Omar creep and be done with it." She picked up her clothes where she'd tossed them and put them on over her swim suit. "Do you have any other choice, really?"

"No," Ahmed admitted slowly. "I guess I don't. You make it sound so simple, so black and white." He followed her to where Nutmeg was tethered and took the lead as Beth led the horse out of the quarry.

The path wandered along the quarry wall.

"This place is really loaded with ghosts," she commented as they walked. "Mom said the Indians came here for religious ceremonies. There's an old gold mine over there," she pointed. "It's abandoned now. Has been for years, and it's pretty dangerous. There's deep shafts. Joey's dad died here." She took a deep breath, remembering. "And then the artesian well is here too. The water trucks drive along the rim there," she pointed again, "and pump the water up. It's too hard to get to the well through the gully."

"We have places like this in my country," Ahmed commented. "It is almost as though they are chosen sites. If you believe in spiritual things, places like this would be called battlegrounds."

Once they reached the lane, Beth let Ahmed ride behind her on Nutmeg's back. He only complained once. "Bareback would be more comfortable," he moaned.

A half mile up the lane, Beth saw King tied to a tree. She headed Nutmeg into the woods and dismounted. "Come on," she invited. "I have a feeling we're going to need help. Joey knows this area like the back of his hand. He's probably as much at home around here as you are on your sand dunes. He's part Indian, you know."

"A nomad," Ahmed observed as he followed her into the forest, "like me."

As Beth expected, she found Joey in his favorite hideout, a copse hidden in a tangle of brush and trees. When Ahmed saw Beth on her hands and knees, crawling through an imperceptible hole in the brush, he shook his head, gathered his robes and followed.

"What do you want?" Joey snarled when he saw the intruders. Furball sat beside him and growled quietly when Ahmed entered the sanctuary.

"Ahmed needs some help," Beth explained. "And don't be a crab. He really does." She grabbed the map and star from Ahmed's hands and explained the job Jorge had given his young charge.

"So what do you figure?" Beth asked when she was finished. "It's not a whole lot to go on."

Joey toyed with the star. "And you don't know what these packages are?" He looked at Ahmed.

"It is not necessary that I know. Only that I do the job. There are others from my country who will come and take care of the rest. But," he glanced at Beth. "I have decided not to call for them yet."

Beth looked expectantly at her friend. "So what's your plan?"

Joey reached into his cache of food inside a hollow tree trunk and passed around candy bars. He munched as he thought. "Our plan," he corrected. "What was your itinerary?"

Ahmed had to think. "The train wreck changed all that. We are here on a cultural exchange."

"Coeur d'Alene was your first stop in Idaho?" Joey pressed.

Ahmed nodded. "I was to tour the horticultural gardens. They had a gift to present."

"When?"

"Monday," Ahmed recalled. "At one in the afternoon. I thought I should cancel. That is, until Jorge told me about the star."

"Nope," Joey declared. "You don't cancel. You go, as planned. And you wear your get-up. I'm betting you'll come home with more than a plant."

Chapter 3

Ahmed attended church with Beth and Joey the next morning. He made quite a stir in the congregation when he entered the small church in his colorful flowing robes and sat beside Beth.

Chuck preached a simple sermon to his small congregation. He talked about the life of Christ in a way Beth had never considered before. "He was made perfect by the things that He suffered," Chuck said. "And He was obedient to death, even to the death of the cross."

Ahmed listened respectfully, but Beth noticed he did not join in the prayers.

On the drive home, Chuck commented on the sermon. "You have to understand that the word *perfect* better translates to the word *mature*. I guess its another way of saying that Jesus didn't step into His role as the Christ without paying a price in His own human life."

Ahmed seemed to withdraw into himself and stared without seeing out the window.

After riding in silence a few minutes, Chuck made a suggestion, "Perhaps you should consider calling this trip off."

Ahmed shook his head. "No," he said quietly. "I am not finished here yet."

Lunch was hectic. Ahmed opted to take his meal in his room after Eva almost hit him with a mound of potato salad. The young mother, Linda Trevor, was a paragon of patience and self-control. "Eva really is a darling child," she said to Ahmed by way of apology. "Once you get to know her."

"I shall hope to be spared that honor," Ahmed said coldly.

When the kitchen was clean, Beth changed into her baseball uniform. Her red hair, now in pigtails, stuck out from under her cap, and her cleats made clicking noises as she walked across the hardwood floors.

"Come on with us," she called as she pounded on Ahmed's bedroom door. "You can't sit around here all day."

Ahmed was startled by the change in her appearance. "*You* are playing the baseball?"

"Sure," Beth nodded. "But you can't show up at a game in that outfit. Haven't you got some regular clothes, you know, like denims?"

When Ahmed shook his head, Beth ran down the hall and disappeared up the narrow attic stairs

...at led to Joey's bedroom. She rummaged through his drawers until she found a new pair of denims she knew were too big for the boy.

"Here you go," she said triumphantly when she handed them to Ahmed. "Now you can look normal."

Ahmed almost smiled and some of the sadness of the last few days faded from his face. When it was time to go to the ballpark, he even chose to sit in the back of the truck with Beth and Joey rather than in the cab with Chuck.

Beth chattered nonstop all the way to town. Joey sat with his back propped up against the cab, methodically slapping a baseball into his glove.

"Chuck can explain the game to you," Joey said as they neared the playing field. "It can't compete with politics, but it's fun."

Once they were parked, Joey hopped out of the back of the truck. "Hope you're not too bored," he said.

As soon as Joey stepped onto the playing field, he was in his element. He and Beth played a game of catch until other players arrived, then Beth found herself without a partner. The only other girl on the team was absent. In fact several players were missing. As the rival team took the outfield to warm up, Joey quickly counted heads.

"Coach Parker," he yelled. "We're short!"

The coach, a middle-aged man with the look of an athlete gone to seed, flipped through his clipboard of papers and pushed his glasses up on his nose. "There's nine players," he called back.

Smiling, Beth walked out on the field from the dugout and stuck her tongue out at Joey when she passed him on her way to right field.

Joey stifled a groan, shifted the wad of bubble gum in his mouth and threw some warm-up pitches.

The game went well until the third inning. Joey's team was ahead by two points when disaster struck. Bobby Campo, the shortstop and probably the best player on Joey's team, came up to bat. He managed to hit the ball over the second baseman's head and seemed sure of at least a base hit. But when the center fielder fumbled the ball, Bobby decided to run for second base.

"Go back!" Beth screamed from the sideline.

Tubs Malone was playing second base for the opposing team, and he eyed the running boy with malicious glee. He was standing just off the base, ready to catch the throw from center. When the ball came, it was wide. Tubs reached for it and managed to swing back over the baseline in time to collide with Bobby who was going down for a slide.

Bobby literally bounced off the bigger boy.

"You're out!" the umpire yelled. Bobby didn't move.

Beth stopped yelling and Joey ran out on the field.

"Time!" Joey shouted, making the signal with his hands as he ran. Coach Parker came out of the dugout and trotted across the diamond to the injured player.

Tubs hovered over the group, fingering the ball and looking sheepish. Finally Bobby sat up.

"Let's get him off the field," Coach Parker said. Joey helped as they half carried the dazed player to the sidelines.

"What happened?" Bobby moaned.

Joey glared at Tubs. "You ran into a wall," he replied.

When Bobby's dad came out of the stands and led his son to their car, Joey fumed. "Great! Just great! They knew they couldn't beat us fair! Now we'll have to forfeit!"

The umpire approached Coach Parker. "Look, this isn't the major leagues; we're just a little county ball club. You drum up another player, substitute, whatever and we'll go on. That was a pretty lousy play and they owe you one, so it's up to you."

Coach Parker shrugged. "We could barely field nine players as it was."

"Wait a minute!" Beth piped up. "Is it too late in the season to draft new players?"

Parker shook his head. "The last day for signups is this Wednesday."

Beth grinned and trotted to the stands. She stood in front of Chuck and Ahmed and looked expectantly at the foreigner. "You game?"

"What?" Ahmed stammered.

"We need you," Beth said. "All you've got to do is stand on the field and stop the ball if it comes to you. And you have to bat if it's your turn, but don't worry about that. I never get a hit either."

Joey walked up behind her. "You might get dirty," he warned. "And you probably wouldn't be much good, but at least we'd get to lose the game fair and square."

Beth gave Joey a dirty look and turned back to Ahmed. "Please? We're going to help *you!*"

Joey walked back to the dugout and sat down to take off his cleats. Ahmed glared at him. "I will play," he announced.

Beth whooped and led him to the umpire. "This is Ahmed. We're putting him on the roster." Then she took him to the dugout and found him a spare glove and a cap.

The umpire went to his position behind the catcher. "Let's finish this game," he bellowed. "Batter up!"

The teams jockeyed back and forth for the lead. Beth got on base once on a walk, mainly because she was so afraid of striking out she refused to swing at anything. Ahmed struck out twice. He connected with the ball a couple of times, but fouled it far left.

"You straighten that out," Beth consoled him, "and you'll be dynamite."

By the bottom of the ninth inning, Joey's team was in the field and ahead by one. Joey was pitching to the best of the opposing team's batters and was clearly worried. He tried to strike out the first batter, but the boy connected and hit a liner down to third.

The next batter hit over Joey's head. Beth had the presence of mind to stop it and simply tag her base for the forced play, but she didn't have the nerve to try for a double play at first base. She figured if she threw the ball wild, Joey would undoubtedly kill her.

Joey walked the next batter and when their cleanup hitter came to the plate, Joey deliberately walked him too.

Beth couldn't believe it. "Are you crazy?" she whispered loudly. "You loaded the bases!"

"I can see," Joey snapped. He looked grim as he stood on the pitcher's mound and concentrated on his next pitch. Strike . . . ball . . . strike, the pitches came. Joey was certain the fourth pitch was a strike, but the batter hit the ball deep into right field.

Beth felt as if her heart had stopped as she watched Ahmed run to position himself for the catch. He bobbled the ball, but managed to gain control, then, hearing Joey's cries, he threw it to the infield.

Joey caught the throw and whipped the ball to the catcher who tagged the runner attempting to score from third base.

The game was over.

"You did it! You did it!" Beth screamed. She ran to Ahmed and threw her arms around his neck. "You were great!"

Other players congratulated Ahmed, but it wasn't until the crowd had dispersed and Chuck motioned them toward the truck that Joey approached Ahmed and proffered his hand. "You did good," he said simply. Ahmed returned the glove, but kept the cap.

"I'll give this to my son one day," he said on the drive home. "And I'll tell him how his father played the American baseball."

"You planning on getting married soon?" Joey asked.

Ahmed looked solemn. "I am betrothed now. My father arranged it last year. I will wed next summer."

Beth wilted but Joey was kind enough not to notice.

"You people sure marry young," Beth said finally and then remained silent the rest of the way home. She suddenly felt very young and very plain and very foolish.

The next morning during breakfast there was a knock at the front door.

"There's a man here from the railroad," Chuck told the group seated around the table. "He'd like to speak with all of you."

Mrs. Hazelton and the Trevor family moved into the parlor.

"I'll get Ahmed," Chuck said to Beth. "You take coffee to the parlor. There's time before the school bus comes."

Chuck was surprised to find Ahmed's bedroom door open. The young man was standing at the window staring out at the front yard.

"I expect the railroad will offer you some compensation and provide a way for you to continue your trip," Chuck explained to his visitor, "if that's what you want to do."

"I've decided to stay," Ahmed broke in. He faced his host. "You may act as my intermediary. Decline any funds except those to pay for my stay here, of course."

"I wish you'd let me call the State . . . "

Ahmed silenced the man with an impatient gesture. "Thank you. I am fine." He dismissed Chuck and returned to his contemplations. But before Chuck could reach the door, Ahmed added, "I need you to drive me to Coeur d'Alene at one o'clock. I have an appointment at the horticultural garden."

Chuck ventured to argue. "I think you ought to have some sort of official escort. You're not just another tourist, you know. I'd feel a lot better . . . "

"If you don't wish to accompany me, I can make arrangements to travel alone. I am in no danger.

Our countries are not at war," Ahmed said impatiently. "When I am ready for an official escort, I will summon men from Shamir. Until then, I am capable of making my own decisions. I know of no reason for you not to respect that."

Chuck sensed there was more to be said, but Ahmed's silence was impenetrable.

The Idaho State Horticultural Gardens covered four acres of land on the outskirts of Coeur d'Alene. Chuck parked the truck, pocketed the keys and looked nervously around the partially filled parking lot. "I don't fancy this bodyguard business," he admitted as he opened Ahmed's door.

Ahmed's robes whipped in the wind as he strode purposefully to the entrance. The receptionist noticed them immediately and summoned the proprietor. A pair of newspaper reporters jumped to their feet and hurried to take photos of the meeting.

"Have your plans changed since the accident?" one reporter asked. "Have you been called home?"

Ahmed smiled graciously. "My plans remain as before. My father believes I am capable of continuing as planned."

The group grew as they toured the gardens. Chuck hung back and watched carefully. At the end of the walk, the proprietor led Ahmed to a garden coffee shop.

Chuck declined to sit at the same table and kept watch of the other patrons. He hardly noticed the man who served the honored guests.

The waiter was an older man of oriental descent and was professionally inobtrusive as he filled cups and removed plates. Even Ahmed was unaware of his presence. Only a slight touch on the arm alerted Ahmed to the man's quiet, but quick move. Ahmed felt something drop into his lap. As the conversation at the table continued, he reached down and felt a key. In a casual gesture, he tucked it into a pocket in the folds of his robe.

A gift presentation was made, complete with photographers. Ahmed accepted the rare plant, and allowed Chuck to carry it to the truck. Later, as they drove away, Chuck breathed a sigh of relief. "I hate to question your judgment, but this business makes me nervous."

Ahmed held out the key. It had a metal disc attached with the number 5 engraved on it. "Where would this go?"

Chuck slowed the truck and took the key. "Where did this come from?"

"I must know where it *goes*," Ahmed insisted. "I do not pretend to understand everything. Suffice it to say that I have some business of Jorge's to attend to. I am afraid I need your help and your promise to be discreet."

Chuck searched the young man's face. "You're sure you're doing the right thing? Going it alone like this? A simple phone call and you'd have all kinds of help."

Ahmed took the key back. "Your assistance should be enough. Of course, you can refuse."

Chuck sighed and pulled into a supermarket parking lot. "Let me see that key again." He turned it over in his hands several times. "Well, a locker, probably a public one. I don't know. Yes, I do!" He tossed the key back to Ahmed and drove back onto the street. "I bet I know!"

He drove to downtown Coeur d'Alene and pulled into the bus station. Ahmed followed the young pastor inside to a wall of small lockers. Chuck took the key and tried it on the locker marked 5. It fit.

Chuck and Ahmed exchanged glances and Ahmed stepped forward to open the door. Inside was a shoe box sized package wrapped in brown paper. Ahmed was surprised at its weight.

Once they were back in the truck, he set it on the seat. He remained silent and preoccupied during the drive to the boarding house.

"Aren't you going to open it?" Chuck asked as he drove.

"No," Ahmed said after a long pause. "Jorge said only to turn it over to a friend, a man I will summon, Professor Omar. I must contact Omar now that I know there is something here for him."

When they arrived at the house they saw a strange car parked outside. Chuck found Beth lying on the living room floor watching television, with a half empty bowl of popcorn in front of her.

"Two guys came and Mrs. Hazelton left. I think she took some towels," she reported. "She must have cleared out while I was at school."

"Where'd you put the men?" Chuck asked.

"In the green room," Beth replied.

"Beth!" Chuck exclaimed. "That was Jorge's room! He died in there!"

"Yeah, I know," Beth grinned. "I don't like them."

Ahmed shifted the package in his arms. "That room is adjacent to mine. Who are these men?"

Beth stuffed her mouth with popcorn. "Hunters," she garbled. "Deer, I think. They're after deer." She didn't take her eyes off the television.

"I thought deer season didn't open for another month," Chuck murmured as he headed for the kitchen.

Ahmed walked toward the back stairs that opened off the dining room. "Beth," he whispered, "I'd like to speak with you in a moment."

Beth waited until Chuck was busy then scrambled up the parlor stairs to Ahmed's room. He had changed into the blue jeans and motioned Beth into the room without a word. After he shut the door, he led her to the closet and pulled the heavy box off the shelf.

"You got it!" Beth exalted. "What is it?"

"Shhhh!" Ahmed hushed her. "I need to hide it. I would feel better until the professor arrives. Is there a place in the house?"

"A place? Man, I can find a hundred places!" Beth whispered excitedly. Her brow wrinkled, then she motioned for Ahmed to follow her. She tiptoed down the upstairs hall to the storage chamber. The room was filled with excess furniture, crates and empty boxes. Beth made a path to the far end and then disappeared in an opening along one wall.

"Hand it here," she said softly. The weight of the box was more than she anticipated and it smashed her fingers against the floor.

"There's a crawlspace under the eaves here," she said when she pulled her fingers out of her mouth. "Nobody'll ever find it."

Ahmed nodded his thanks. "I am unsure of what is the right thing to do," he admitted. "I'm glad you are helping me."

Beth blushed, but Ahmed did not see. He glanced uneasily down the hall at the hunters' room. "I think I must call the professor now."

Chapter 4

Linda Trevor became Chuck's best friend when she offered to take over the cooking chores for the remainder of their stay. She fed the children early that night and put them to bed before serving the adults a meal that began with fruit salad and ended with baked Alaska. The husband, John, was more relaxed than he had been since their arrival.

"We're from Seattle," he told the others. "I'm in the military and just got a big promotion." He looked at his pretty wife, who was beaming with obvious pride. "And I got a new assignment. This trip on the train was a pretty sorry attempt at combining a vacation with moving."

"You survived," Chuck pointed out. "I think

you've got much to be thankful for."

"Yeah, I guess so," John agreed. He held Linda's hand. "I've got the best the world can give a man." He turned to Ahmed. "I was real sorry to hear about all your trouble. I have to admit I never thought I'd ever meet anyone from the Middle East that I'd like. You people sure know how to give the world a headache."

"Well," Chuck added, "just because some nations in that part of the world have leaders we don't like, doesn't mean they're all madmen."

Ahmed smiled. "My father is not a madman, I can assure you. He withstood great pressure even from within our country to begin peaceful interaction with America. My trip here, as inconsequential as it seems, is the first step in—how do you say it—breaking the ice."

"Does your schedule include a stop in Pocatello?" Linda asked. "Or anywhere near it?"

One of the hunters, who'd introduced himself as Mr. Martin, leaned forward in his chair to hear Ahmed's answer.

"I believe so," the young man answered. "I believe there is some sort of military installation near there, am I not correct?"

John Trevor nodded. "That's where I'll be. You ought to stop by and see us. Eva seems to have taken a liking to you."

Linda laughed. "She doesn't throw her food at just anybody."

"I'm surprised your government didn't call you home, what with that train wreck and all," Mr. Martin remarked. "You must have some pretty important things to do in the States."

Ahmed's face was closed. "Peace, Mr. Martin, is

always worth pursuing."

Mr. Martin pushed away from the table. "Well, I never did get much involved in politics," he admitted. "Too messy for my tastes. I prefer less bloody pursuits."

"Like hunting down defenseless animals?" Joey asked, not even trying to hide his feelings.

The man looked back at Joey from the foot of the stairs. "Yeah, like hunting."

Beth curled up her lip as she watched the man disappear upstairs. "You know how people sometimes remind you of animals?" she asked. "Well, that guy reminds me of a buzzard."

"What do I remind you of?" Ahmed asked with a twinkle in his eye.

"An eagle," was Beth's quick reply. She blushed when she realized what she'd revealed about her feelings for the stranger.

"What about me?" Joey asked.

Beth looked at him carefully and weighed the effect of her answer before giving it. "A buck, only you don't have all your antlers yet."

Beth helped Linda with the dishes then wandered outside to find the guys. The days were lengthening and the air was warmer. Sounds of hammering drew her across the south pasture to the creek. Thanks to the rains, there was water running again over the stones, gurgling down the bed on its way to Lake Ponderay, two miles away.

Joey was in a tree with nails sticking out of his mouth and a hammer stuck in his belt. Ahmed was handing planks up to him one by one until Joey had eight of them piled on the two support planks already nailed in place.

"What are you doing?" Beth asked. "Aren't you

a little old for a tree house?"

"Call it what you want," Joey answered around the nails. "I'm not sleeping in that house one more night with those babies screaming at two o'clock in the morning." He set a plank in place and deftly nailed it down. "It's nice up here," he added. "And quiet."

"What's wrong with your place down the lane?" Beth asked.

"Nothing, if you don't mind walking a mile." He nailed another plank in place. "I thought I was going nuts last night."

"What if it rains, Smarty?" Beth pressed as she watched the platform take shape.

"I've got my canvas," Joey said, pointing to the bundle at the base of the tree. "I'll be just fine."

"I have never done anything like this," Ahmed admitted.

"That's 'cause you don't have rocks in your head," Beth told him.

Martin did not go to his room after dinner. He stopped at the head of the stairs and listened to the dinner conversation continue downstairs. Then he moved quickly to Ahmed's bedroom and slipped inside. His search was fast, careful and thorough. His trained eye was able to see that he had returned everything to its original place. He was troubled that his search revealed nothing. He stood in the center of the room trying to find some spot he'd failed to check. Then he took a small electronic device from his pocket and inserted it in the lamp beside Ahmed's bed.

He listened at the door before leaving and quickly returned to his own room. Once his door was locked, he took a small case out of his closet, removed the earphones and adjusted the dials. Satisfied with his work, he concealed the radio receiver and laid on his bed to begin his wait.

Martin's partner, Randolph, returned later that night and nodded his approval at the receiver. "Anything in the room?"

Martin shook his head. "I know we're not supposed to touch his highness, but that kid is trouble. I can feel it. Have we got a line on what's been smuggled in?"

"Not yet."

"Did you fix the phone?" Martin asked.

Randolph nodded. "The tap's on. The next move is theirs."

When Joey's platform was built, he condescended to let Beth and Ahmed climb up to join him. The branches of the tree provided a screen on three sides. The fourth, overlooking the creek, was more open. The gurgle of the water below and the rustling of the leaves blended into a peace-filled song. A thought flitted through Beth's mind as she sat very still and listened. *Maybe the world isn't totally out of control after all.*

"Time for a summit meeting," Joey declared when they were settled. "Beth told me you got a package."

Ahmed nodded. "One of five," he said and pulled the map and star out of his shirt pocket. "Our original schedule was for a visit tomorrow to Crown Cove. There is an Indian museum there."

"And a burial ground," Beth inserted. "Weird place. We went a couple of months ago."

"What time?" Joey asked as he moved the star

so that the second point lay on Crown Cove.

"Eight o'clock in the evening. There's going to be some sort of tribal dancing. It is the time of year for one of their religious ceremonies. I understand very few people are permitted to witness it in its entirety."

Joey nodded. "I know. The next stop, according to the way this star falls, is Timberline, Sand Bar, then De Long, then some spot out in nowhere. That's strange," he mused. "I wonder what's out there?"

Two other heads bent over the map. "I used to let Jorge handle all of those details," Ahmed told them. "I never bothered to ask about such things. I knew he'd brief me as we went along."

"Royalty!" Joey shook his head in disgust. "What would you do if you didn't have servants to do your thinking for you?"

"Exactly what I'm doing now," Ahmed replied solemnly.

Joey's team played another ball game Tuesday afternoon. He made several quick-thinking plays, but in the eighth inning, while their team was at bat, Beth lobbed a fly to the third baseman who not only caught it, but also threw out the runner who could have scored the winning point. Joey's team never got another man on base and lost the game.

Ahmed, in one of his tailored suits did not play and, afterwards on the drive to Crown Cove, sat in the cab with Chuck. His arrival at the Indian museum was again recorded by newspaper reporters and cameras. Beth and Joey, who'd both been to the museum before, found the tour much more interesting with the Indian guide.

The dinner, a tribal affair, was held outside. Chuck, Beth and Joey were ushered to blankets on the edge of the group while Ahmed and his guide sat with the chief and his family.

Beth looked suspiciously at the strange food set before her. "I heard once that Indians ate raw worms," she said.

"This is some kind of corn dish, Beth," Chuck explained patiently. "It has some seasonings and bits of meat. That's all."

"What kind of meat?"

"Dog," Joey supplied as he ate his second spoonful.

Beth pushed her dish away. "I'm not hungry."

Joey chewed with exaggerated enjoyment. He rolled his eyes and smacked his lips as he took more.

Beth swallowed hard and looked away.

When the fish came, Beth picked at it. But the well-cooked fish, eye still attached to the head, seemed to follow her every move. By the time the fresh fruit was served, she had lost all of her appetite. She wondered at Ahmed, eating everything set before him and listening graciously to his host.

"I'm glad I'm not him," she commented to Chuck.

"And this is nothing," Chuck said. "His position carries some terrible responsibilities. I wonder sometimes if he realizes that."

Beth and Joey exchanged glances. "I think he does," Joey replied. "At least a little bit."

The reporters were asked to leave after the meal, and due only to Ahmed's intervention, Chuck, Beth and Joey were allowed to stay for the ceremony. The drums began a slow beat, and two male dancers jumped into a small circle drawn in the dirt. Their faces were painted and their costumes were adorned with long, beautiful feathers.

"They look like birds," Beth whispered.

"That's what they are," Joey replied softly. "They're telling a hunting story—from the hunted's point of view. My mom told me a lot of the Indian legends when I was little. This was her tribe, you know."

"What are they doing now?" Beth whispered when the beat changed and the intensity of the dance grew.

"Shhhh!" Joey hushed her. "Can't you see?"

The dance ended with the death of the birds. Beth could follow enough of the drama to understand that much and she felt a sense of sorrow creep over her. The dances and incantations that followed only heightened that feeling.

As the full moon rose over the trees, the fire burning in the center of the circle burned brighter. Chuck touched Beth's knee and whispered. "They don't seem to have much hope, do they?"

Joey turned away from the dance. "We were a hunted people," he said softly. "Mother told me the stories. This time of year is the time of our great darkness."

Beth slipped her hand under Chuck's and was glad for his presence. The girl playing the part of the victim in the next dance gave a shrilling cry and the sound drifted away into the forest.

"She's crying out for help," Beth said, her voice shaking.

"We thought there was none," Joey replied as

once again the drama told them that the darkness triumphed.

When the dancing was over, the old chief slowly rose to his feet and lifted his arms to the sky. His half-sung soliloquy was a prayer of supplication, a cry to the moon and the silence of heaven.

When he was finished, no one stirred. No one spoke. The silence extended even into the forest.

A cold chill rippled goose bumps across Beth's skin.

Slowly the spectators disappeared. Ahmed bowed deeply to his host and joined his friends again at the museum gate. "Their religion is savage and wild," he commented softly as they walked to the truck.

"And sad," Beth added, unable to shake off the cold.

"In the fulness of time . . . " Chuck whispered, thinking.

"What happens then?" Beth asked. "Do all the lights go out? Do we all get sucked into the darkness?"

Chuck shook his head. "No. There's a Bible verse that goes, 'When the fulness of the time came, God sent forth His son . . . . ' It's hard to understand sometimes why God allows the darkness so much power." He opened the door of the cab for Ahmed.

"Our religions are similar in many ways," Ahmed noted. "We worship the same God, although we differ on the question of Jesus and Mohammed. But, tell me, Mr. Warren, why do you think God tolerates evil?"

"Perhaps it's for our sakes," Chuck replied.

"How's that suppose to be good?" Joey asked. "I

thought God was suppose to love us."

"He's given us the means to withstand evil and the strength to fight it. Maybe fighting that fight and winning is part of the reason for our existence." Chuck helped Beth into the back of the truck. "I don't pretend to understand everything in the spiritual world and I sure don't presume to know God's reasons for everything. Greater theologians than I have debated this issue for centuries."

"Maybe understanding why there's evil isn't as important as standing up to it," Beth offered.

Chuck pulled the blanket from behind the seat and tossed it to Joey. "Let's go home," he said.

Beth shivered as they drove, in spite of the blanket pulled up around her chin. They were in Cooper's Creek when she was warm enough to realize she was starving. She knocked on the back window of the cab and yelled her request. Chuck understood enough of her desperate gestures to pull into the hamburger stand on the edge of town.

"You haven't lived until you've tried American junk food," Beth exclaimed to Ahmed as she jumped out of the truck.

They were sitting at one of the outside tables consuming french fries and hamburgers when Joey realized what had been bothering him. "No one contacted you," he half started, half asked Ahmed.

The young man shook his head. "I kept expecting something, but, no, nothing. Perhaps we figured it wrong."

"What?" Chuck asked.

"Another package, like the last one," Beth offered.

Chuck looked at his young charges and noted the air of conspiracy between them.

"It's no big deal," Beth persisted. "When Ahmed's friends come from Shamir, they'll take over. We're just helping out 'til they get here."

Chuck's face was stern. "If you don't call your professor friend tonight," he warned Ahmed, "I'm calling the State Department. That's a promise. I don't like this solo business of yours and I like it even less now that I know these two renegades are involved with you." He turned to Beth and Joey. "Have you ever thought that maybe you were meddling in international business?"

"Ah, Chuck," Joey protested, "if it was any big deal, they wouldn't have sent Ahmed."

When Joey realized what he had said, he tried to rectify his error. "They wouldn't send the crown prince on a dangerous mission, would they?"

Joey's question went unanswered as a racing car whipped down the street, its tires screaming. Seconds later another car, chasing it, raced through town. Every person in the hamburger stand rushed to the street to watch.

"They're gonna kill somebody," one woman said. "Fool kids!"

Tires screeched as the first car swerved in an attempt to make a corner. Then there was a tremendous crash as it failed and struck a concrete wall.

Chuck ran toward the wreck followed by others in the crowd. Beth hung back, afraid of what she'd see. Joey and Ahmed stayed close to the front of the running group. The second car saw the accident and did not even pause. It tore straight ahead down the road and disappeared.

"Somebody call an ambulance!" Chuck shouted when he reached the car. "And get back! It could go up!"

He could see the driver trapped behind the wheel. The front of the car was pressed like an accordion against the wall. Chuck wrenched the door open and the man's dazed eyes rolled up to look at him. When he opened his mouth, strange gutteral sounds came out. The garbled words sounded strangely familiar.

"Ahmed! Come here, quick!"

The young prince hesitated only a moment, then ran to the car. He knelt beside the dying man and murmured a few words Chuck did not understand.

The man tapped the last reserves of strength and replied. Chuck was right. It was the language he had heard in Jorge's hospital room.

"My coat—pocket . . . " the man said. They were his last words.

A siren's whine grew louder. Ahmed's shaking hands rummaged through the man's blood-soaked clothes. Fire erupted in the engine and Chuck pulled on his arm. "We've got to get back! The gas tank will blow!"

Ahmed felt a slip of paper and wadded it in his fist as he allowed Chuck to pull him away from the burning car.

An ambulance and a small fire truck arrived and men immediately sprayed the fire with white foam while others attempted to get the driver free. At the first sign of spreading fire, they gave up and ran. The explosion knocked them to the ground.

Ahmed hung his head and began the same plaintive chant Beth had heard coming from his room the day Jorge died. It reminded her of the old Indian chief's supplication to heaven. She felt the cold again and tried to shake it off.

"It's winning, isn't it?" she said to no one in particular as the car became a funeral pyre.

"What?" Joey asked.

"The darkness," she said and climbed into the back of the truck and pulled the blanket around her.

When the sheriff's department arrived, Chuck was among the witnesses who were thoroughly questioned. Even Ahmed was asked if there had been anything said to help them determine the man's identity and the reason for the high speed chase.

"I had never met the man," Ahmed told them. "And I . . . I do not know why he was being pursued."

"What did he say to you?" Chuck pressed. "He said something just before the fire broke out."

Ahmed would meet no one's eyes. He stared at the charred remains of the car. "You would have to understand the deserts of Shamir. It is an eternal disgrace for a man to die with his work undone."

Nothing more was said about the accident, not even when they arrived at the boarding house. Ahmed, in response to Chuck's ultimatum placed a call to the University of Camil in Shamir, to Professor Omar. Nearly an hour passed before the operator called back with the international connection. This time Ahmed took the call.

The conversation on the phone was short. Chuck had to trust that Ahmed spoke the truth when he said that the professor and his assistant would arrive the following Saturday.

"No sooner?" Chuck asked, obviously displeased with the delay.

"There is some trouble at home. He did not elaborate, but he cannot begin his flight until Friday. But he directed me to continue with my tour. If you would escort me, I am certain my father would appreciate that at least part of my trip would be successful."

"I'll do all I can to help you with the tour," Chuck said, "but I think you ought to let your professor friend collect any official packages."

Ahmed did not respond and Chuck could not tell if his silence was agreement or simply a refusal to make a promise he knew he would not keep.

The house was quiet and dark when, hours later, Ahmed slipped out. He walked purposefully to Joey's platform by the creek.

Joey woke with a start and scrambled for his flashlight.

"It is I," Ahmed said when the light struck his face. "I must talk with you." He climbed to the platform and Joey made room for him on the sleeping bag.

Ahmed pulled a rumpled piece of paper from his pocket. "I do not know what this is," he admitted as he handed it to Joey. Joey smoothed it out and read the blurred printing with difficulty.

"The man in the car?" he asked.

Ahmed nodded.

"It's a dry-cleaning ticket," Joey said. "For a place in Coeur d'Alene."

"I do not think Chuck will take me," Ahmed said. "Would you go?"

Joey looked at the paper, then at Ahmed. "Yes."

"How will you get there? Coeur d'Alene is far from here."

Joey flicked off the flashlight. "I don't know. I'll figure something out."

The two youths sat on the platform without speaking. The differences in age and background seemed unimportant. Finally Ahmed climbed down. "My father is wise to want the friendship of your people," he said.

Chapter 5

Beth and Joey caught the bus to school at 7:30 the next morning. At a stop a mile past the boarding house, Joey got off.

"You're going to get in trouble," Beth said as he rose to leave.

Joey just looked at her and shrugged his shoulders.

"Good luck," she added.

He walked to the highway and waited for a county bus. When he arrived in Coeur d'Alene, he found the street address of the dry cleaners on the ticket Ahmed had given him.

When he got there, he handed the crumbled slip to the woman at the counter.

"Looks like this thing went through the war,"

she said as she smoothed it out. She pushed a button that moved the pulley to the number on the ticket and pulled a man's suit off the rack.

Once he'd paid the bill and walked outside, he moved quickly out of view of the cleaner's window, pulled off the plastic covering and rummaged through the pockets. He found what he was looking for inside the vest pocket. At first he didn't know what the paper stubs were for. The initials *ICA* were in bold type and then there were a series of numbers. "Idaho Central Airlines?" Joey mused.

He ditched the suit in a clothing bin for a charity organization and wandered along the street. Suddenly it came to him. "Luggage!"

Joey turned around and headed south out of town; the county airport was on the outskirts of the city. He had another three miles to go when a rancher with a load of hay slowed and offered him a ride. Joey sat on a bale of hay in the back and counted the money he had left.

Enough to get back to school, he figured.

Once inside the small airport terminal, Joey handed the claim ticket to an attendant behind the ICA counter. The woman brought a white overnight case out and set it down with a thud.

"Your sister must have bricks in here," she commented.

"Yeah," Joey muttered as he picked it up. "Girls!"

He caught the county bus back to Sand Point and walked onto the high school campus in time to go to his gym class. He made room in his locker for the case and covered it with his dirty sweat suit.

After school, he found Beth. "You've got to carry this thing," he said as he handed her the heavy case. "I'd look pretty dumb carting it across campus."

Beth needed two hands to lift it and finally gave her books to Joey. "Everybody's going to think we're going together, if we keep this up," Beth teased.

Joey snorted. "Nobody's *that* stupid!"

Beth considered dropping the case on Joey's foot. "I sure do wish I knew what was in this," she said. "And I wonder why that guy Jorge, didn't just ship this stuff over with their other things."

"Maybe he didn't have it," Joey offered. "Maybe this trip was his cover to collect it."

Martin was at his bedroom window when the school bus stopped in front of the boarding house. His expression became thoughtful when he saw the case in Beth's arms. He ground out his cigarette and put away the radio receiver before going downstairs.

He found Joey with his head in the refrigerator. "Where's the girl?" he asked.

"Huh?"

"The girl."

"Did you need something, Mr. Martin?" Beth asked from the door to the old kitchen. Two piles of books lay on the dining room table and Beth's hands were empty.

Ahmed came down the dining room stairs in a hurry and popped into the room. "Did you . . . "

"School was fine," Joey said loudly. He started pulling food out of the 'fridge. "We've got another game tomorrow. You want to play?" Joey ignored

Martin as he waited for Ahmed's answer. Ahmed looked quickly at the man and hesitated to speak.

"Bobby's dad won't let him play," Beth added. "We need you in right field. You want some melon, Mr. Martin?"

The man's face tightened. "No thanks," he said and left the room.

Joey watched him. "You're right, Beth. That guy's a buzzard."

"Did you get it?" Ahmed whispered.

Joey nodded and Beth motioned for the two boys to follow her. She led them through the old kitchen with its long-handled pump on the sink and the cast iron wood stove to a heavy wood door in the west wall of the room. Beth pushed the door open with her shoulder.

"This is the cool room," she explained to Ahmed. "In the old days, before they had refrigeration, they used to bring in big hunks of ice and then keep the meat and dairy products cool in here."

The room was small and rectangular. The walls were made of heavy, hand-chiseled blocks of stone. A ledge, also of stone, ran around the perimeter of three walls.

A large, black steamer trunk sat against the back wall.

"We put your trunk in here when it came," Beth explained. "The day Jorge died. It was too heavy to carry upstairs and everything was so confused, I forgot to tell you."

Ahmed nodded. "I wondered where it was. It belonged to Jorge."

"I put the new package," Beth pushed aside a pile of empty cardboard boxes, "here."

"That's two," Ahmed said as they left the cool room. "Tomorrow is Timberline. I think I am to be interviewed at a television station. I will have to look in Jorge's appointment book."

The trio walked outside and drifted toward the creek. They climbed to Joey's platform and Ahmed once again opened his map and set the star in place.

"I wonder," Joey mused. "Maybe Chuck's right. Maybe you ought to have some kind of escort. Maybe you're not as safe as you think you are."

"Your government knows I am here," Ahmed said. "And they have not sent anyone. Apparently they see me as of little importance."

Randolph returned to the boarding house that evening along with a thunder storm which was blowing across the Canadian border. Each time Beth saw lightning she'd count the seconds until the clap of thunder. When she couldn't even say "one" she knew the lightning was directly overhead.

The second time the lights flickered, Chuck went to the old kitchen and found the kerosene lanterns. Eva, her thumb stuck firmly in her mouth, followed Chuck wherever he went. Determined to be prepared, Chuck placed a lamp in each of the occupied bedrooms and set two each in the parlor, living room and dining room.

A crack of lightning erupted simultaneously with an explosion of thunder that shook the old house. The lights went out moments later. Somewhere close something exploded. Chuck ran out the front door and saw that a large electrical transformer attached to the top of a telephone pole had been directly hit by lightning. Sparks were shooting out of it as if it were a Roman candle on the fourth of July. The guests congregated in the parlor. Eva started wailing and the young parents were hard pressed to quiet her as well to soothe the fussing babies. Beth tried to pull the little girl onto her lap, but Eva would have nothing of it and ran instead to Ahmed. He didn't quite know how to handle the situation, and Beth wondered if the young prince had ever held a small child in his arms. She had to smile when Eva curled up in his arms and snuggled her curly head against his chest.

Joey opened the piano lid and found a piece to play. It was from Beethoven's Ninth Symphony, but the calm beauty of the music seemed meager defense against the cacophony outside.

Chuck came in from the porch. "I've never seen a storm this fierce," he said. "At least there's no danger of fire. I thank God we've had some rain or these woods would be going up like tinder."

John and Linda Trevor walked the floors with their little ones while Ahmed sat still with Eva on his lap. Mr. Martin stood behind Ahmed and stared out the window at the storm.

"Not such good weather for hunting," Ahmed observed for lack of other conversation.

Martin seemed angry and tense. "Not necessarily," he replied.

───────

Later that night, Randolph and Martin sat together in their room in the dim light of their kerosene lamp. The electricity had not yet been restored though the storm had quieted to a heavy downpour.

"It galls me to think we have to protect that kid," Martin admitted. "He's nothing but a bloody terrorist."

"We're not absolutely sure of that," Randolph reminded him.

"I don't know why we can't just haul him in and be done with it," he said.

"The big boys say no. They want to catch the skunks red-handed and discredit their whole operation. If that kid thinks he's got press coverage now, wait 'til this thing breaks. Besides, there's an outside chance he's just being used."

Martin laughed. "Sure. And I'm the King of England."

Just before dawn, a private jet landed at the Coeur d'Alene airport. Three men disembarked and were met by a black Mercedes. In a matter of minutes the car was waved through a gate far from the terminal and sped toward the city.

Inside, an obese man removed his gold-rimmed glasses and rubbed his small, inset eyes. His jowls were heavy, and despite his naturally dark skin, he had a sickly pallor.

"This is coming along nicely," he said to his companions. "The boy is working out well. If he is caught, the disgrace will be his father's. If he isn't, we'll finish the job with very little involvement ourselves."

"And what happens to Ahmed then, Professor?" one of the men asked.

"He will be a liability to our cause," Professor Omar stated.

The two men understood his remark. "It is not wise to touch the heir," one of them ventured.

Professor Omar glared at him. "It is more dangerous not to."

They rode in silence until they reached a small hotel overlooking Lake Coeur d'Alene. "For the present, you two must see that the Americans do not interfere with Ahmed's chores."

"What if he opens one of the boxes?"

Omar smiled. "He is too obedient a son to do that."

A telephone call early in the morning precipitated a hasty departure for Randolph and Martin. They came downstairs dressed in hunting fatigues and carrying high-powered rifles. They declined Linda's offer of breakfast and rushed out to their car. Only Martin hesitated a moment to stare at Ahmed. The young man was giving Eva a piggyback ride and the little girl was laughing wildly.

Joey, who'd opted to sleep under a roof that night, met Beth as she was about to descend the stairs to the dining room. She was wearing her high-heeled pumps and a multi-layered outfit.

"Where're you going?" Joey asked. "Halloween's a long ways off."

"School," Beth answered with nonchalance as she carefully descended to the dining room. "Oh, and by the way," she added. "When I play second base tonight, I will *not* be getting out of your way so you can make all my plays."

"Who says you're playing second?" Joey asked as he thudded downstairs behind her. "I was thinking Ahmed should play infield."

"Joey!" Beth howled. She spun around to attempt a quick kick to his shin, lost her balance and ended up entering the dining room backwards and teetering wildly.

Joey laughed. "You're gonna be so lame from those dumb shoes you won't even be able to walk by this afternoon. I'm doing you a favor!" Beth swallowed her anger when she noticed Ahmed watching the exchange. She went to her chair and allowed Ahmed to pull it out for her. Joey shook his head, straddled his chair and dug into the bowl of scrambled eggs.

"You're the one with rocks in your head, Beth," he said.

Another telephone call that morning confirmed Ahmed's visit to the local television station in Timberline for the scheduled interview. He dressed carefully in western clothes and was lying on his bed staring at the ceiling when Chuck came to get him.

"I have greatly inconvenienced you," Ahmed said when he noticed Chuck's polished appearance.

Chuck was surprised by this new thoughtfulness in the young man. He waved the comment aside. "I'm glad to help."

Ahmed swung his legs over the side of the bed and stared out the window.

"You're very tired, aren't you?" Chuck asked.

"I need very much to talk to my father," the young man answered. "But I have a job to do here. I'll see him when it's over."

"Jorge's death was a blow," Chuck offered. "You've carried on very well." He paused, hoping to see some light in Ahmed's face. "All the news coverage has been very positive. Your trip has had a good effect upon American opinion of you and your people."

Ahmed sighed and slowly stood up. "I hope so. Otherwise Jorge would have died for nothing."

Chuck and Ahmed dropped John Trevor off at the railroad station near Timberline before going on to the television station. John was already two days late reporting to his new post at the military base. He shook Ahmed's hand as he said good-bye.

"You have a beautiful family," Ahmed said. "You are a very fortunate man."

———————

The television studio was set up to look like a garden patio. In addition to the host of the talk show, there were several newspaper reporters present to ask questions.

Ahmed handled himself with diplomacy and an air of self-confidence that amazed Chuck. One woman reporter asked few questions and seemed satisfied to simply take notes. After the taping of the program, she left quickly, taking a large purse and tucking her tape recorder under her arm.

When Ahmed and Chuck left the station she stepped out from behind a car and walked with them. "Where is the old man?" she asked nervously.

Ahmed was startled and stopped walking.

"No! Please, go on to your car," she urged.

"He's dead," Ahmed answered as he went. "I am, ah, conducting his business for him."

The woman pushed a strand of hair away from her face. Chuck noticed that her hands were shaking.

"Who is this man?" she asked.

They reached the truck and Ahmed nodded for Chuck to leave them. "A friend," the young man said. "I trust him."

The woman hesitated, glanced around the lot, then reached into her handbag. She pulled out a satchel and was handing it to Ahmed when she noticed a land cruiser parked beside a utility repair truck at the edge of the lot. A man sitting inside was watching their every move.

The woman thrust the weighted satchel into Ahmed's hands and, without another word, hurried away in the opposite direction from the observer.

Ahmed joined Chuck in the cab of the truck. "I don't like this," Chuck began as he drove out of the parking area.

Ahmed's cry interrupted him. The young man had glanced back to watch the woman and saw the man in the land cruiser drive quickly after her. The woman ran.

"What now?" Chuck asked, trying to see while still keeping the truck on the road.

The woman disappeared into the woods next to the parking lot and the man's vehicle careened to a stop just off the pavement. The driver jumped out and ran after her. Chuck stepped hard on the gas pedal, then took a sharp right turn and raced down the road beside the wooded area where the pair had disappeared. Both he and Ahmed saw the woman jump into a black Mercedes as the pursuing man pulled a gun from his coat. The powerful foreign car pulled sharply into traffic and the man was left staring at his elusive prey.

The ride to the boarding house was tense. When they pulled up behind the house, Chuck took a deep breath and started to speak.

"I know," Ahmed stopped him. "If you believe you must call your State Department I cannot stop you. But, Mr. Warren, I know *I* am not in danger. And I believe there is more at stake here then we realize. I also know my father is an honorable man."

He pulled the paper-wrapped parcel out of the woman's satchel. "The men from my government will be here soon. Until then, I ask you not to intervene."

He stepped out of the truck with the package under his arm and waited for Chuck to join him. "I think the traitors from Shamir, the ones Jorge mentioned, are here now. They want to stop me and it only makes me more determined to succeed. Surely you can understand that." He laid a hand on Chuck's arm and it was the first familiar gesture he'd ever given the pastor.

"Help me, please," Ahmed asked. "If I fail in this simple thing, how can I ever rule a nation?"

Chapter 6

That afternoon Martin and Randolph were summoned to Coeur d'Alene. A big man with gray crew-cut hair stood in the small hotel room with his back to his subordinates. Smoke from his cigar filled the darkened room with a blue haze. "You failed to intercept the woman," he stated.

Martin fidgeted. "She was picked up. We didn't know they had support here."

"She was valuable," the man said. "We could have determined the exact nature of their plan. She would have told us everything."

Martin looked to Randolph for help. "They haven't called in the boy. He's still operating," the older man said.

"Hummmm, yes, unfortunately," the big man said, turning to face his men. His eyes were as cold and sharp as needles. "For you. Whatever's coming down is still working. But," he ground out his cigar, "the vultures are gathering."

"Do you want us to take the boy out?" Martin asked.

"No. This is going to cause enough havoc without getting the Shah's son caught in the crossfire."

"He's part of the operation," Martin insisted.

"He's untouchable," was the man's last word and when he once again turned his back on them, the two men knew their conference was over.

When Beth and Joey arrived home after school, Ahmed turned the third package over to Beth without saying a word. When Beth watched him climb the parlor stairs, he seemed old and weighted down. Her feet hurt too much to even try to think of a place to hide it, so she just stuck the package under her bed and resisted the temptation to open it.

As Ahmed walked down the upstairs hall to his room, he noticed a strange piece of cloth sticking out of the hall closet. When he opened the door, he found Eva sitting on the floor with her special blanket clutched in her fist, and a thumb securely planted in her mouth.

She looked up at Ahmed solemnly, her big blue eyes meeting his. Ahmed smiled and squatted down. "Are you hiding from someone?"

"The monster," she said around her thumb. "He came in my nap, and my daddy's not here to make him go away, so I hided."

Ahmed awkwardly pushed one of her tangled locks of hair out of her eyes. "I think you had a bad dream. Does that happen very often when your daddy's gone?"

Eva nodded her reply.

Ahmed lifted her up and carried her back to the family's bedroom. He tapped lightly on the door and when there was no answer, peeked in.

Mrs. Trevor was asleep on the bed with the younger children asleep on either side. Ahmed held a finger to his lips and carefully carried Eva to a little cot that stood near the windows.

"Is this your bed?" he asked in a soft whisper.

Eva nodded, her thumb a definite impediment to speech.

Ahmed laid her down and pulled the covers up over her little body. "If you promise to go to sleep, I promise not to let any monsters come near this room," he said.

Eva smiled. "Honest?"

"That's what handsome princes do for a living," he replied. "Didn't you know that?"

Eva giggled. Her eyes stayed on him as he tip-toed to the door. When he looked back at her, her eyes were drooping, and he was feeling strangely at peace again for the first time in a long time.

———————

Joey made good his threat to Beth at the ball game and had Ahmed play second base that afternoon. Beth steamed as she limped to right field. By the end of the second inning she wished she'd brought her nail polish along so she could have had something to do.

The other team was ahead by four points when Tubs Malone hit the ball to left field. He was barreling down the baseline to second when the fielder shouted to Ahmed to get ready for the throw.

Tubs grinned when he saw Ahmed position himself right on the base. Ahmed paid no attention to the runner, concentrating only on making the catch. It would have been a close call, if he'd caught it. But just as the ball reached Ahmed, Tubs hit him full on, causing him to go sprawling. Joey ran for the loose ball, rolling in the infield, and glared at Tubs.

"He was blocking the baseline," Tubs stated innocently. "You know that's illegal. You guys have the dumbest basemen in the league."

Ahmed got to his feet, retrieved his cap and started dusting himself off. "You Americans play rough," he said to Joey. "I'd hate to be at war with you."

Joey helped him brush off the dirt. "We don't *all* cheat," he said pointedly. "Old blub belly there will get his, one of these days!"

Tubs was playing second base in the eighth inning and when Beth, who'd finally made a hit, led off from second, she made certain she stepped on his foot. "Great cleats, huh? They really help you dig into the *dirt!*" Beth made it home on a steal. It was a close play. She had to dive for home plate, and no one was sure if she'd made it in time.

"Safe!" the ump called.

When Beth stood up, her front half was brown with dirt, except for the gashes on her arms and the huge scrape on her knee that was trickling blood down her shin.

Ahmed, next up to bat, helped her limp back to the dugout. "Is winning worth all this?" he asked.

Beth's eyes were two white circles in a brown

mask. Despite her mangled body, she was grinning. "Yep! It sure is!"

Joey's team was now only behind by one point. Ahmed took a few practice swings with the bat, took a deep breath, then stepped into the batter's box. He and the pitcher locked eyes, then the boy on the mound concentrated on the catcher's mitt and wound up for the throw.

"Strike one!" was the call.

The pitcher smiled.

Joey led off from first.

Ahmed caught a piece of the next pitch and fouled it right. "Strike two!"

"Watch the ball!" Joey shouted. "It's just you and the ball!"

"All you have to do is meet it!" Beth yelled. She refused the coach's offer for first aid and was watching the action on the field.

The next pitch was low and outside. Joey stole second. Ahmed almost swung at the fourth pitch, but caught himself in time. "Ball two. Two balls, two strikes."

The pitcher took his time. The pitch was high and inside. Ahmed had to jump back to keep from being hit in the head. He looked at the pitcher and saw malicious satisfaction in his eyes. Ahmed's lips tightened and he gripped the bat harder.

Beth held her breath as the pitcher wound up. The throw was fast and straight. Ahmed swung and connected. Beth knew from the sound of leather on the wood that it was a solid hit.

Ahmed took off for first and Joey raced for third. The ball soared to left field and the two outfielders ran back in an attempt to catch it.

They collided as the ball flew over the fence.

Beth screamed and jumped up and down. The people in the stands were on their feet cheering Ahmed around the bases. Joey tagged home and waited for Ahmed to finish his circuit. The dark-skinned boy laughed as he stepped on home plate and took Joey's outstretched hand. It was the first time anyone had ever heard that sound coming from his lips.

Beth ran out of the dugout and tackled him with a hug and a juicy kiss. "You're great! A home run! I've been playing for a year and I've never hit one yet!"

The other players on Joey's team welcomed Ahmed back to the dugout as the game continued. Tubs' team got one more run, but couldn't pull it together enough to take the lead away.

"That new boy, on second, he does all right," a spectator commented to Chuck.

Chuck felt a sense of pride he couldn't explain. "Yeah, he's okay," he said.

Other observers, however, felt differently. Two men standing beside a black Mercedes parked on a side street watched the game through binoculars. They spoke their own language and their conversation was terse.

"He is easily corrupted," one of them said.

The other one snorted in disgust. "He plays games at a time like this! Jorge was right. That family is not fit to rule!"

Another observer was stationed on a bluff overlooking the playing field. Martin had binoculars too, and watched not only Ahmed, but also carefully scanned the people in the stands.

When the game was over, he stood up and prepared to leave. He walked to his car, then on a sudden impulse used the binoculars to check the entire area beneath him. That's when he spotted the black car.

He whistled softly. "Omar's here!"

The next morning Mrs. Trevor received a call from her husband. "Pack up the kids and come on home!" he said. "The house is ready. I'll meet you at the depot in Pocatello."

Chuck helped load her luggage into the car she'd rented and offered to take her to Timberline to catch the early morning east-bound train. Ahmed carried Eva to the car and strapped her under the seat belt. Randolph watched from the upstairs window.

"You'll look us up, won't you?" Linda asked. "If you're coming to Pocatello, you must stop by. Eva thinks you're her special knight in shining armor."

Ahmed took Eva's chubby hand, bowed and kissed it. "Good-bye little princess. I'll see you again," he promised.

They were not gone more than fifteen minutes when the telephone rang again. The voice spoke the desert language. "Come to the chapel in Sand Bar, at two o'clock." Then the line went dead.

Ahmed set the receiver down slowly. His face tightened and the look of age that Beth had seen settled once again upon him. He found the keys to Chuck's truck and then went to the south porch and sat down on the bench swing. Beth and Joey, ready to leave for school, found him there, his eyes closed, rocking slowly. The morning breeze was working itself into a gusty wind and the sunlight filtering through the trees beside the house anointed Ahmed's bowed head with intermittent shafts of light.

Beth and Joey hesitated to interrupt the moment. The wind brought clouds, seemingly from nowhere, and the light disappeared. An untimely darkness enveloped the house and Beth shivered. Only the light inside the house now staved off the gloom. When Beth could stand it no longer, she climbed the porch steps and touched Ahmed's arm. "Let's go inside."

He raised his head slowly. "I must go to Sand Bar to a chapel. I am afraid."

"We'll go with you," Joey said. He took the keys from Ahmed's hands and threw his books down on the swing.

Joey started the truck with no problem and drove out of the driveway with relaxed assurance.

"We're gonna get killed for this," Beth said. "Ditching school is bad enough, but taking the truck . . . Chuck will go into orbit." She was sitting between the two fellows, her knees drawn up close to the seat to stay out of the way of the gear shift.

"I've got my permit," Joey reminded her. "Besides," he glanced over at Ahmed, "we're on state business."

In 20 minutes, they were in the small community of Sand Bar. It was a rustic country town with a flavor of the 1800s. Its nostalgic atmosphere had been carefully preserved by the farsighted town councilmembers who realized it would attract a certain number of tourists on their way to Coeur d'Alene.

The chapel, a small wood building near the center of town, had a spacious graveyard behind it filled with headstones dating back to the first regional settlers. A stream ran through the quiet resting place, and there was a duck pond in the center of the tree-filled yard. It was a hushed place.

Ahmed took the lead as they walked inside the church. Beth hung back, looking at the stained glass windows which depicted various events in the life of Christ. The crucifixion window was in the front of the church.

There was no sign of anyone else in the place. Ahmed's slow walk down the aisle ended at the pulpit. As he took the first step toward the empty crucifix a man in a priest's robes stepped through a side door and beckoned him into an adjoining room.

"Wait here," Ahmed directed Joey quietly.

The man closed the door and went to a small chest sitting on a table in the center of the room.

"You are being followed," the man said at last. He lifted a package out of the chest and placed it in the young man's hands. It, like the others, was rectangular and heavy. "Be very careful."

Ahmed re-entered the sanctuary and beckoned for Joey and Beth to follow him outside. Instead of returning to the truck, he entered the cemetery and made for the center of the shaded enclosure.

There were several benches scattered along the paths. He sat on one and looked at his two new friends. "I must know now what this is about. Something is wrong."

He pulled the wrappings from the package and let them drop on the ground. When the last scrap was off, they saw a wooden box, finely carved.

"Help me open it," he asked Joey.

The two boys were pulling the tight-fitting top off when they heard a strange cry, then a shot.

Beth heard the zip of the bullet only a split second after the report of the gun. It reminded her of the lightning strike after the thunder.

"Run!" she screamed.

Joey grabbed the box and the three of them took off in different directions.

Two men ran after them. They let Beth go and concentrated on Ahmed and Joey. Beth ran to the truck and was nearly there when she saw Randolph, a walkie-talkie in one hand and a revolver in the other, racing into the cemetery.

More shots were fired.

Beth huddled down in the cab of the truck and prayed. She heard men shouting and more gunfire. The cab door opened with a jerk.

"Don't shoot! Don't shoot!" she screamed.

"It's just me," Joey said as he climbed behind the wheel and pushed the box under the driver's seat. "They have Ahmed," he added as he fumbled with the keys.

"You're not going to leave him! What are you doing?"

Joey started the truck. "We're going to get help and then we're going to hide that package. They could've shot us, but they didn't. I don't think they'll hurt him."

"But Joey!" Beth tried to catch sight of Ahmed, but all she saw in the cemetery was two men running through the trees, one of them holding his arm, and Randolph in pursuit.

"We're no match for what's going on here," Joey said, his voice wavering. "Chuck was right."

He backed the truck up and spun out of the parking lot in a shower of dirt and pebbles. When they arrived in Cooper's Creek, Joey stopped at the

Kootenai Cafe and phoned Chuck at the boarding house.

"Where in heaven's name are you? And where's my truck?" Chuck fumed.

"I can't explain now," Joey hurried to say. "But Ahmed's in trouble. Those hunters, Randolph and Martin, they chased off two thugs up in Sand Bar. But they're not hunters, Martin's not a hunter."

"Get home!" Chuck commanded. "I'm going to do what I should have done days ago. I'm calling the State Department."

But despite Chuck's words, Joey didn't go straight to the boarding house. He continued on the lake road.

"Where are we going now?" Beth asked. "Aren't we in enough trouble already?"

Joey steered the truck off the road. "I'm not handing that box over to just anyone, Beth. Those men back there, they didn't want us to open it. Whatever Ahmed's collecting, it's pretty important. Maybe *he* ought to decide what becomes of it.

"Wait here," he ordered and he took the box with him into the woods. Fifteen minutes later he returned. "Okay," he said as he started up the truck again. "Time to face the music."

Chapter 7

Omar's anger was black. The two wounded men who reported to him that night ended up wishing their injuries were more serious.

"He was opening the box," one of them explained.

Omar sat at a table in the hotel suite and drummed his fat fingers on the wood. "The Americans have him now?"

Their silence was enough of an answer.

"Get out!" he hissed.

Omar sat thinking for nearly an hour. Then he left the hotel, found a pay telephone and made a lengthy and expensive call.

———

Chuck's anger was silent. He took the keys

from Joey once the truck was parked behind the house and walked away without saying a word.

Beth and Joey found him in the parlor.

"If that lad is hurt . . . " Chuck said. He sat on the edge of the couch and stared into the cold, empty fireplace. "I shouldn't have ever let him call his own shots."

A car drove into the driveway, followed by two nondescript sedans. "Martin!" Chuck observed angrily as he watched them come. "He sure has some explaining to do!"

They parked the cars behind the house. Ahmed stepped out of one of them and was immediately flanked by Randolph and Martin. Four more men from the other cars formed a semicircle behind him.

Ahmed's face was closed and angry. He strode to the house with two of the men staying close behind.

Randolph reached in to his coat pocket and pulled out a slim wallet for Chuck to see. "CIA," he said. "I'm Officer Randolph and this is Officer Martin."

Chuck took the wallet and read the credentials carefully before handing it back.

"So you were here all the time," he said. "Mind telling me what's going on?"

Randolph pocketed his wallet, his eyes constantly moving, checking the area. "We have reason to believe Ahmed is in grave danger," he hesitated. "I can't tell you much more than that right now. His visit is sanctioned by our government. That gives him special privileges."

Martin directed the other two agents to concealed stations in the yard. Then the two "hunters" headed for the house. Beth and Joey tagged behind, trying to be unobtrusive, listening raptly.

Chuck went to the telephone in the dining room.

"What are you doing?" Martin demanded.

"Checking out your story," Chuck replied.

Beth and Joey exchanged glances. Martin crossed the room and took the telephone receiver out of his hand. "No. You'll have to trust us. There's more to this than we can tell you." He noted the suspicion in Chuck's face.

"Consider yourself under house arrest," Martin said.

Later that afternoon Beth was summoned to Ahmed's room. She'd been helping Chuck put the house back in order; they worked together, quietly returning the breakables to the tables and mantles where they'd previously been in danger of Eva's inquisitive fingers.

"We'll need to clean the house before your Mom and Paul get back," Chuck said as they worked. Joey stayed at the piano with Furball at his feet and fumbled through assorted pieces of music.

Martin came down the parlor stairs and called Beth. "He asked for you to bring up some coffee," the man said.

Beth prepared the silver tray and managed to get it upstairs without slopping very much. The agent stationed outside Ahmed's room tapped on the door.

Beth heard the lock being opened before Ahmed spoke. He was stiff and formal until the door was closed again. "Thank you," he said as he took the tray out of her hands. He made some unnecessary clinking noises with the cup and saucer, then took Beth's hand and led her to the closet.

"We can talk in here," he whispered.

"We can talk out there!" Beth countered.

"I don't think so. Listen," he urged. "I asked them if I could call my father, and they won't let me. I don't think they are whom they say they are."

"Those creeps! They can't keep us prisoners! This is America," Beth fumed.

"Whoever they really are," Ahmed went on, "I think they are engineering an incident, something to embarrass my government."

"But why?"

"It doesn't matter why. I have a plan. Professor Omar is coming Saturday and things are going to change when he gets here and sees what's going on. Even if these men are really from your government, I doubt we'll be free to move about. We'll probably just finish our trip and then be escorted out of the country."

"So?" Beth asked. "That's not so bad, is it?"

"I need to get the last package and deliver them all to Omar. At least then I will have kept my promise to Jorge."

"Martin isn't going to let you out of his sight," Beth said. "You couldn't even get to the front door!"

"You can," Ahmed said. "You and Joey."

"But . . . "

Ahmed led her out of the closet. He had stripped the sheets off his bed and he showed Beth one of his robes that he'd tucked inside the sheets. "Joey," he whispered and he handed her a slip of paper.

"I'd like the laundry back by tomorrow afternoon," he said loudly. "And I will take breakfast in my room in the morning." He winked at her as he loaded the sheets in her arms and opened the door.

Beth didn't even look at the man in the hall. She carried her load to the old kitchen where the washer and dryer sat in a corner and stuffed the entire bundle into the washer. Then she went to find Joey.

"He's down at the creek," Chuck told her. "I wouldn't be surprised, though, if someone was watching him." The young pastor was using the vacuum as he spoke, and the noise from the machine covered their conversation. "Beth, this business is over for us now. You know that, don't you?"

Beth noted the worry and the warning in his voice and nodded.

"I'm coming up," she announced when she arrived at the base of the tree. "We got trouble."

Joey was sitting on his sleeping bag playing, absent-mindedly, with a twig. She handed him the slip of paper Ahmed had given her. "The University of Idaho in De Long, today at seven o'clock," Joey read aloud. "Meet the president of the Student Coalition for Peace in the Middle East, at the fountain in quadrangle. Wear the robes. I feel certain that the last package will be delivered to you there."

"Oh, great!" Joey exclaimed. "Can you see me traipsing around in that get-up?"

Beth shrugged. "*He* can't go."

"This'll never work! What if this president guy

talks that gobbledygook to me? I don't know the language!"

"Stare at him," Beth offered. "Act imperial, you know, like Ahmed did when he first got here."

Joey broke the twig into small pieces.

"I've got the robes hidden," Beth told him.

"I'm scared of this thing now," Joey admitted after a lengthy silence.

"Me too, Joey. But he needs our help. We promised we'd help him."

Joey sighed. "Okay, put 'em in the saddlebags. We'll take King and Nutmeg for a ride. There's a basketball game at school tonight. Tell 'em we're going there!"

"You think they'll let us?"

"We won't know 'til we try. I can't figure out who's the good guys and who's the bad guys any more. Seems to me like everybody involved in this thing is lying."

"Except Ahmed," Beth added.

"Yeah, except Ahmed," Joey agreed. "But, that's what scares me."

Beth took the saddlebags to the house and filled them with food and a heavy jacket. She waited until no one was around before she went to the washing machine and retrieved the robes. She folded them carefully and pushed them into Joey's bag.

"I'm on the team," Joey told Martin when the man objected to their leaving. "If I don't show up for the game, somebody's gonna come out here and find out why."

Chuck was surprised when he heard that Beth and Joey were being allowed to leave. "Be home before ten," he directed them. His eyes looked tired, his face, drawn. There had been some tense moments during lunch.

Chuck had broken out in uncharacteristic anger. "You can't just hold us here indefinitely! I have a right to some legal counsel, at least."

He'd gone to the telephone, and this time Martin had pulled the cord right out of the wall. "You don't have any rights, not at the moment," Randolph said. "We're operating in the interests of national security."

Chuck wasn't impressed. "Which nation?"

"I'm sorry you people got involved in this, Mr. Warren," Martin said. "But you're not going to be allowed to interfere, nor are you going to be put in any danger. These two kids can go to their game, but they have to understand that if any whisper of this business gets out, you'll be held responsible."

He'd looked at Beth and Joey sternly and both of them nodded. "We understand," Beth assured him, her head bobbing up and down.

———————

Martin and Randolph met early that evening in their room. Randolph prepared for some much needed sleep. "They'll make a move soon," he said as he unstrapped his shoulder holster. "Whatever their scam is, they'll try to pull it together in the next 48 hours."

"At least we know now that Omar's in the country. He'll show up soon. It'd sure be nice to nail him."

"We've got nothing on him, Martin. Take it easy. As far as we're concerned, that guy's an angel of light."

———————

When Beth and Joey arrived at the crossroads, Beth continued on to school and tethered Nutmeg in a grassy area where other horses also grazed. Joey took the road to De Long. He hid King in some trees far off the road, then thumbed a ride to the university. He carried Ahmed's robes in the shoulder pack he normally used for his books.

He'd never been on the university campus before, and he felt somewhat cowed by its size and by the throngs of students hurrying from one building to another for evening classes. The fountain sat in the center of a large quadrangle. Joey found it, then went into one of the buildings and found the men's room. He locked himself in one of the cubicles and changed into Ahmed's robes. He stuffed his own clothes in the shoulder bag, fixed the head piece and used part of the sash to cover his face. "Brother!" he muttered. "I don't believe this!"

He heard some other students enter the restroom so he flushed the toilet before letting himself out of the cubicle. In spite of the staring eyes that followed him, he tried to act normal as he walked out.

The robes kept getting tangled up in his legs and Joey had to stop twice to pull them free. The sash fell out of place so many times that Joey finally just held it in place. He needed it more for camouflage than to complete his disguise.

When he reached the fountain, he sat on a bench near some bushes. He stashed his knapsack under the bench and hoped he was inconspicuous.

Time dragged, and only the sight of other foreign students in native dress made it bearable.

When a young dark-skinned man changed directions to walk straight toward him, Joey tensed.

The young student touched his forehead and bowed, murmuring a greeting Joey did not understand. Joey rose to his feet and gestured with his hand. "Today we speak the English," he growled in a deep voice.

The student apologized profusely.

My name is Gilbar," he said. "Come, before you speak to our group, I must first show you the campus." He looked around. "Where is your escort?"

"I sent them away," Joey said, again forcing his voice octaves lower. "I tire of them."

The student looked at him with curiosity and Joey stiffened. He willed his eyes to be angry and met the student's eyes. Joey stared him down.

"Of course," the young man said. "Excuse me. There will be members of the press to interview you after your address," he went on. He looked at his watch. "But there is time!"

Joey's heart beat wildly. *Press conference? Address?*

"Is there something wrong?" the student asked.

Joey grunted and motioned for Gilbar to lead the way.

First they went to the library, a huge, multi-level building with sky lights and plants growing in an atrium in the center. Joey listened to the tour guide monologue and kept his responses to grunts and nods.

Their next stop was the bookstore. Gilbar showed him the shelves of books on the Middle East and talked at length about the classes the university offered in global politics.

"We are most anxious to hear your views on armaments for the gulf states." He lowered his voice. "We personally feel the Americans will sell anything, if the price is right. Even their integrity."

Joey almost blasted him with a rebuttal, but caught himself in time. "Yes," he growled. "It is very sad."

Gilbar looked surprised. "Sad? It plays right into our hands."

They passed through the cashier's station and Gilbar stopped suddenly. "Your briefcase," he motioned, pointing to a wide leather case on a set of shelves just inside the door. "You must not forget your case."

Joey almost corrected the error, then realized it was no mistake. He nodded, and pulled the briefcase off the shelf. A letter was taped to the handle. Joey stuffed it inside his robe and followed the guide outside.

"Now to the student union. We begin in fifteen minutes."

Sweat broke out on Joey's brow. The case was heavy and he gripped it tightly. "I must excuse myself a moment," he said.

Gilbar nodded. "Of course. The facilities are down the hall."

"Go ahead," Joey urged, his voice low. "I must have a few minutes alone."

Gilbar lowered his eyes, bowed and went to the elevators. "Third floor," he called back. "Fifteen minutes."

Joey gulped and nodded. His knapsack and clothes were halfway across campus under the bench near the fountain. He made a quick decision. He saw an exit at the back of the building, and trying not to hurry, he walked outside. He strode purposefully toward the side street and only turned around when he heard a shout behind him. Gilbar was standing on a balcony on the third floor. Several other students stood beside him.

Joey ran. He lifted the robes with one hand and held on to the briefcase with the other. "This is the end," he panted. "Ahmed, old pal, this is absolutely it!"

When he reached the city street, Joey flagged down a bus and climbed aboard. The bus had already started to move when he realized all his money was back on campus in his jeans.

"Ah, I'm broke," he confessed to the driver.

"Trick or treat, eh?" the elderly black man replied. "Okay friend, off at the next stop."

Joey swallowed his embarrassment and took the seat nearest to the door. Everyone on the bus was looking at him, and a pair of girls across the aisle giggled openly.

Joey was only too glad to disembark at the next stop. He held the briefcase under one arm, hitched up his robes and started walking. He tried to stay off the main thoroughfares, realizing he'd be easy to spot if Gilbar decided to come after him. If there had been any way to ditch his new outfit, he would have, but all he had on underneath was his underwear and running shoes. As soon as he reached the edge of town, he left the road and went deep into the woods. The going was slower, but at least he wasn't being gaped at by every passing motorist. After what seemed like hours he reached King. He tied the briefcase behind the saddle and started for Sand Bar to meet Beth.

She had just come out of the gymnasium and was walking toward the snack bar when a hand yanked her into a custodian's closet. She tried to scream, but a hand clamped over her mouth. "Shhh!" Joey ordered.

"What happened?" she gasped when she caught her breath.

"I got another package," and he pointed to the briefcase on the floor, "but I lost my clothes."

Beth giggled as she considered the wonderful possibilities for blackmail. "You've got a problem!" she teased.

"Come on Beth! Help me! I've got to get something to wear!" He sat on the briefcase. "Go find one of the guys on the team and have him get my sweats out of my gym locker."

Beth loved it. She yawned. "I sure am tired of playing right field all the time," she mentioned, her hand on the door knob.

"Beth!"

"Sally Parsons told me today she's writing for the school paper now. She said she needed a good story."

"Okay, Beth Cooper, you play infield," Joey surrendered.

Beth smiled and tore a strip of paper out of her notebook. "Give me your combination," she said. "I saw Bobby heading for the snack bar."

After she found their short stop, she went with him to the gymnasium. "Joey asked me to get them so they could be laundered," she explained.

When Bobby came out of the boys locker room, he handed her the sweatsuit and nodded. "Too bad he waited so long to take these things home," he said. "The whole basketball team nearly fainted when I opened his locker."

Joey was still waiting in the janitor's closet. Beth tossed in the clothes. "I don't think Chuck's going to let you in the house," she said, wrinkling up her nose. "There're laws against air pollution these days."

"It sure beats wearing a dress," Joey rebutted. "Here, stick these things in your saddle bags." He threw the robes at her. The envelope fell on the ground. Beth picked it up and put it in her purse.

Beth and Joey's arrival home was hardly noticed. They rode the horses directly to the stable, and as soon as they turned the corner behind the house they saw a long gray limousine parked near the back walk and three black Mercedes stationed nearby. Four men in dark suits waited beside the vehicles.

"Whoa!" Joey exclaimed as he swung off King's back. "Things are cooking around here now!"

He helped Beth unsaddle the horses and brush them down. As he finished up, Beth took Ahmed's package out of her saddlebag and buried it in the grain bin.

When they entered the house, they heard an argument raging in the parlor.

"This is an outrage!" fumed an obese, bald-headed man in glasses. A diminutive man with a small pointed beard and gray hair stood beside him, obviously unable to follow the English conversation.

"By what authority have you restrained Ahmed?" the heavy man continued, addressing Martin and Randolph. Chuck sat on the couch watching the confrontation and Ahmed stood beside the mantle.

When Joey and Beth entered the room, Ahmed looked at them expectantly and seemed relieved when Joey nodded.

"I am going to protest this illegal and unprecedented aggression! Do you realize, sir, that our ambassador is in Washington right now, meeting with your President?" the new arrival continued.

Randolph held up his hands. "Professor Omar, please! We had reasons, good reasons to believe that Ahmed was in danger. We only acted to protect him until you arrived."

Omar glared at the other man, and each, in his own way, masked his true thoughts.

"Our only concern was for his safety. We know there are subversive elements in your government," Randolph continued. "We thought they would perhaps move against Ahmed while he was here."

"You thought wrong!" Professor Omar snapped. "And now that I am here, your services are no longer required. My men are quite capable of protecting us."

Randolph turned to Martin. "Pack up," he said. "Looks like this assignment is over."

Two dark men who'd come with the professor followed the Americans to their room and silently observed their packing. Randolph was glad the radio receiver for the bug in Ahmed's room was concealed in a suitcase. They checked their things carefully, took their guns from the closet and left.

Randolph stopped in the dining room and spoke to Chuck. "I'm sorry for the inconvenience. You'll be paid, of course, for our board and room."

Chuck accepted the quasi-apology graciously. "At least it's over," he said. "Everything's all right now."

Randolph did not reply. His face was closed to scrutiny and Chuck wondered, as he watched the men drive away, if he was premature in his assessment.

Chapter 8

Beth dressed up for breakfast the next morning. It promised to be a lavish affair. Chuck had her put the best linen on the table and set it with Virginia's finest china and silver. "This is unreal!" Beth whispered as she polished the crystal. "Mom'll never believe this!"

"Unreal, all right," Chuck grunted as he scurried around the kitchen, trying to arrange the pots so they'd all fit on the stove. "I hope these guys like bacon and eggs."

As it turned out, they didn't eat pork at all. Omar and Ahmed sat at opposite ends of the table, flanked by two guards each. The small man, who was introduced as Dr. Neiber, sat beside the professor and did not speak.

Beth and Chuck served them their rolls and fruit, and a disgruntled Joey took his breakfast to the living room and sat in front of the television. "We almost had Ahmed civilized before old butterball showed up," he grumbled when he came back for his third helping.

Beth elbowed him in the ribs and pushed him out of the way so she could take another bowl of fruit to the table. "At least you get to eat," she hissed. "You might save some of that for Chuck and me."

The conversation across the table sounded mysterious to Beth as the older man directed one question after another at the young heir in the desert language.

"And father?" Ahmed asked finally.

"He is well."

"There was trouble."

"Some, but it is under control."

"The Americans said there are traitors."

Omar leaned on the table. "There are people, Ahmed, good people in Shamir who do not always agree with your father. That does not make them traitors."

Ahmed's opinion of that statement showed on his face.

Beth teetered around the table on her high heels. "More rolls?" she asked Omar demurely. He waved her away as though she was a fly.

Beth made a face as she passed behind Omar's chair, then she realized Ahmed could see her. When she looked at her new friend, she saw a twinkle of a smile flicker through his eyes. The guard standing behind Ahmed, however, was not amused.

In the parlor after the meal, Omar allowed Chuck to light his cigar for him, then summoned Ahmed close. They continued speaking their own language.

"The packages Jorge was to receive, you have them? All of them?"

Ahmed nodded.

"Where are they?"

"Here." Ahmed glanced at Dr. Neiber. "Is it not time for me to know of this matter? I have gone to some trouble to complete Jorge's instructions."

Omar stood up. "You will bring the packages to my room."

Ahmed remained seated. "You will tell me first, what they are."

Omar tried to stare the young man down, and though Ahmed occasionally wavered, he would not break. "You forget your place, Professor Neiber," Ahmed said.

Joey interrupted the stand-off. He arrived at the bottom of the parlor stairs with a clatter of cleats on wood, slapping a baseball into his mitt. He was chewing hard on a wad of bubble gum and was wearing his baseball cap. "You coming to the game?" he asked Ahmed.

The look of distaste on Omar's face helped Ahmed make his decision. "Yes, Joey, of course. It will be my last game before I leave. I would not miss it."

Omar's look would have frozen the Amazon River.

"Better hustle," Joey replied. "Game starts at ten."

———————

Ahmed arrived at the ball park in the limou-

sine. Dr. Neiber declined Beth's invitation to come
and retired to his room. Omar, however, and two
of the guards accompanied Ahmed to the stands
and sat behind him. Another guard who arrived
separately, stood far from the bleachers and kept a
roving eye on all movement around the park.

Randolph saw him through the binoculars and
nestled down in the tall grass at the top of the
bluff. "This case is far from over," he murmured.

He thought back to his recent meeting with
Chief Harrison. He and Martin had expected fury,
but surprisingly, Harrison seemed pleased.

"Everything's in place," he said, smiling benev-
olently at his two operatives. "Now we wait. The
exchange will happen soon."

"Do we know for sure yet what we're dealing
with?" Martin asked.

Harrison shook his head. "One source says it's
an arms deal. They've smuggled in some gold bullion and are setting up an arms purchase right
under our noses."

"Sounds wrong to me," Randolph stated. "Why
buy arms here when Europe's wide open?"

"I agree," Harrison said. "But if it's a phony
rumor, then what have they brought in, and why?
We've got a tight network in Europe. If Shamir
went shopping for arms, we'd know and then all
this hullabaloo about peaceful trade would be
washed out. And if," he paused to light his pipe,
"they go to the Eastern bloc, they'd be obligated to
the Soviets. They don't want that. So maybe the
old desert fox has come right into the lair to steal
food. If that's the game he's playing, he has guts,
I'll say that."

"But regardless, we're going to intercept the

exchange, right?" Martin asked. "After all, that was our original briefing."

Harrison nodded. "They've got something. The boy made all Jorge's pick-ups. And we know these men from Shamir are here to make sure no one botches the project."

"One thing I can't figure," Randolph mused. "Our intelligence sources in Shamir told us Omar and his crew are no friends of the Shah. Why would they play such an important part in such a delicate operation?"

"I wondered the same thing. But," Harrison sighed, "the Shah is strong. Maybe they made peace. At any rate, *we* want the old fox to stay in power. We'll interrupt the deal and it'll never make the news. We'll send the boy and the gold back home. The Shah's hands will be properly but privately slapped and the President will go on negotiating peace with them."

Randolph had been silent several minutes. The interview seemed over. "Why did they shoot at the boy in the cemetery? He was opening one of the boxes. Doesn't the kid know what his dad's up to?"

Harrison thought a moment. "Perhaps not."

Martin looked skeptical. "And they would have shot him to keep him from finding out?"

Harrison drew deeply on his pipe. "These nomads are not always rational," he concluded. "Fifty years ago they were crossing the deserts on camels. Civilization takes time."

Randolph shifted his position in the grass and looked over the baseball field. The weapons the guards were carrying were not sticks and stones.

Beth had been promoted to first base. So far she had only missed one throw and that was a wild one from third.

When Tubs Malone hit a grounder between first and second, Beth shagged it and tossed it to Joey who'd run to cover first. "Einstein was right," Joey grinned as Tubs was called out. "The greater the mass, the more energy it takes to move it."

Tubs glared at him.

Matters for the other team got worse as they made one error after another. Joey's team was ahead by 10 points when Beth got a solid hit and sent it to left field. It was the best hit she'd ever made. The first base coach waved her on to second.

"Okay," she panted as she rounded the base and sprinted ahead. Her cap flew off and her red pigtails stuck straight out from her head. The throw from left reached Tubs on second in ample time for him to make the tag, but Beth saw it coming and went down to slide. *So much for my beautiful legs*, she thought as she went skidding through the dirt.

Tubs swung his hands low and hard to catch her. The ball in his fist hit her right in the stomach. Beth was stopped cold and lay in the dirt gasping for breath.

"She's out!" Tubs yelled to the ump.

"Out cold, it looks like," the man said as he trotted out to check the girl.

Joey threw down his glove and ran out on the field. Beth was writhing on the ground, unable to breathe. She was gasping, retching and crying all at once.

"You didn't have to do that!" Joey yelled at

Tubs. He dove for the bigger boy and landed a solid punch in his stomach. In seconds the boys were down on the ground in a tangle of fists. The ump let them have at it while he helped Beth to her feet. Eventually Beth's lungs inflated and she drew in deep breaths. The umpire let the coach help her off the field then turned his attention to the fighters in the infield. Other team players were crowded around the fight, cheering the boys on. The ump waded in. "All right, this isn't a hockey game."

He separated the boys. Tubs had a bloody nose and Joey's shirt was ripped in several places. "I ought to throw you both out of the game," he snarled at them. "Now shake hands and let's get back to the game." The boys glared at one another and stuck out their hands and touched in a gesture of coerced peace.

Beth couldn't play. Chuck took her to the truck and made a pallet for her in the back.

"I think he broke some ribs," she wailed. "I'll probably never be able to have children!"

She was glad to lie down. As she unwound from the tension of the game, she became aware of something else besides the cheering of the people in the stands. The air had a strange stillness, like a vacuum. Clouds blocked out the sun. The field, illumined now by the circle of big lights, sat in the vortex, like an island in the eye of a storm.

The game continued.

Omar sat in the limousine, smoking his cigars, carefully figuring his next moves like a chess player.

The guards kept their posts: two near Ahmed, one at the far end of the park.

Randolph scanned the area from his perch on

the bluff while lightning played between the clouds.

Joey pitched a no-hit inning.

The mother of one of Joey's team players pulled her son out of the game and left the team short one player. "We're in for a storm," she explained over the coach's protests. "I have to get home."

Joey masked his anger and walked to the fence near the stands. He looked at Ahmed and nothing needed to be said. Ahmed pulled his baseball cap out of his shirt pocket and hesitated only a moment before putting it on his head. He took off his suit coat and went out on the field.

When Omar emerged from the limousine and stood by the fence to watch, Chuck sensed there was as much storm in the man as there was in the sky. Joey saw something in Ahmed he could not name and instead of sending him to right field, asked him to play first base.

And Ahmed played. He looked more like an umpire in his good slacks and white shirt, but the baseball cap was his real badge of office. Ahmed filled his position like a pro. Every ball that came his way was caught. Not only did he make the easy catches, but he also thought quickly, saw chances for double plays, and threw straight and fast.

When Tubs came up to bat, the play to Ahmed came from third base. Ahmed stretched to make the catch, tagged the base and stepped quickly out of the big boy's way.

The game was a rout. Joey's team won by 15 points. When they walked off the field after the last out, the whole team was laughing and cheering. Ahmed took off his cap and handed it to Joey.

"Thanks for letting me play," he said.

Joey wouldn't take the cap. "Keep it," he said. "You earned it."

The parking area cleared as the players left. The umpire swept home plate clean, turned off the lights and drove away. The storm swept in to fill the void.

Ahmed walked with Chuck and Joey to the truck, and then with some difficulty, turned away and went to the waiting limousine.

When Beth cleared off her bed that night so she could get into it, the white envelope dropped out of her purse. She had forgotten about it. She put on her robe and started up the parlor stairs to Ahmed's room.

"Where are you going?" Chuck asked from the parlor. He was sitting in the high-backed chair, reading.

Beth handed him the envelope, too sore and tired to wonder if it was the right thing to do. "It's Ahmed's," she explained.

Chuck turned it over slowly. "I thought you agreed to stay out of Ahmed's business."

"Yes, sir, I did."

Someone could be heard coming down the parlor stairs. Chuck slipped the envelope inside his shirt.

Ahmed, looking pale and strained, stepped into the room. "Beth, please get the packages and bring them to my room."

Beth looked to Chuck for permission. He simply nodded. "Do it and then stay out of it. Okay?"

She went to the stable first, then to the cool room. Two boxes were all she could manage at one time, so she made a second trip to the chamber, and once she remembered where she'd stuck it, for the box under her bed.

"Joey's got the last one," she told Ahmed.

A guard went with Ahmed and Beth to the creek. Even though a strong wind had risen and rain threatened to fall any minute, Joey was roosting in his treehouse bedroom. He directed his flashlight at the intruders. "Who goes there?" he demanded. He lowered the light when he saw the rifle in the guard's hand.

"I need the package, Joey," Ahmed stated.

They took the limousine down the lane. Joey left the visitors in the car and went into the forest alone. Furball met him at his secret place.

Joey pulled the package out of the hollow tree and when Furball saw it, the dog growled low and deep. "Think we ought to peek?" the boy asked.

The wolf-dog whined and backed away.

Lightning cracked overhead. The air was heavy and charged with electricity. Joey took off the wrappings. He held the wooden box, finely crafted, tightly sealed. "What do you think?" he asked his dog.

Furball's one good eye blinked. The animal made a sound that was close to pain.

Joey found his knife and used the sharp tip to pry the box open. He lifted out an oblong block of dull-grey metal that was seamed around the edge. He worked on the seam until the crash and cry of the forest in the wind made him so uneasy he stopped.

"It's none of our business," he concluded. He put the heavy metal brick back in the wooden box and hammered the lid back in place. When he returned to the car, he turned it over to Ahmed.

"You were gone a long time," Omar said coldly as he took the box out of Ahmed's hands.

Joey didn't answer. The clouds broke open and a deluge of rain hammered on the car. Joey was suddenly very cold.

Chuck was in Virginia's office when the limousine returned. He had the envelope on the desk and was about to give it to Ahmed when he heard two of the guards carrying something through the parlor. He stood at the door to the office and watched the men maneuver the heavy black steamer trunk up the stairs. Chuck returned to the office and slowly tore open the envelope.

Once they'd delivered the trunk, Omar sent the guards out of the room. Dr. Neiber stood in a corner and stared at the five packages on the bed. "It is time for you to know the true purpose of your trip to America," the professor told Ahmed. "Tomorrow we are scheduled to visit the military post outside Pocatello. We are there only surreptitiously as a gesture of peace. Our true intent, the reason for all of this," and he gestured toward the packages, "is this."

The bulky man went to the trunk, took a key from his vest pocket and opened the trunk.

"Come here," Omar ordered the young man. "And Dr. Neiber, you may leave us. You will have work to do very soon now."

Once the old doctor had left the room, Ahmed looked into the trunk. Inside rested a basketball-sized silver globe with the continents intricately detailed on the surface. It was a beautiful piece of art. At its base was a large wooden box of the finest ebony and carved with intricate figures of eagles in flight. Ahmed was struck by its beauty.

Omar leaned over the trunk and with difficulty lifted both the globe and the box free of the case. He opened the box using a hidden latch. Ahmed saw that it was empty.

"Bring me the packages," Omar directed him.

"I still do not understand," the young man admitted as he complied. He brought the wood covered bars to Omar one at a time and the professor fit them neatly into the ebony base.

"Gold," Omar told him. "Bullion."

Ahmed's eyes opened wide. "Enough to ransom a king!"

"Or outfit an army," Omar added.

"Why is it here?" Ahmed asked, fear entering his voice. "My father knows of this?"

Omar shut the ebony base. "Of course," he scoffed. "There is a trade agreement going on in Washington, oh, yes. Make no mistake. But there is also an arms sale going on in Idaho. This is by far of greater importance."

"But why must we arm Shamir?" Ahmed asked. "Father swore he would never allow us to be pulled into the conflict in the gulf."

"Of course that is his position in public," Omar said. "We have to maintain a position of neutrality as long as we are not armed." He stuck another cigar in his mouth. "We would be fools to do otherwise. But now . . . "

"Tomorrow," Ahmed began to figure. "Tomorrow we deliver this 'gift' to the American military base?"

Omar nodded, smiling.

"And in return?"

"Missiles, guns, ammunition will be delivered

to us by the end of the week in Shamir."

Ahmed sat on the edge of the bed. "But why the secrecy?" If the Americans know . . . "

"Only a very few Americans know. The Americans have their problems too, you see. Our purchase will be delivered very discreetly. The other gulf states must not know."

Ahmed paced to the window. The rain beat on the glass and made the night seem forbidding.

"Father has never played false before, never."

"You are no longer a child, Ahmed. Your father acts for the best of Shamir."

Ahmed shook his head and wished he could make the wind stop blowing.

Downstairs Chuck sat in the office staring at the sheet of paper before him. He did not understand the written words, but the diagram was easy to understand for anyone familiar with munitions. It was instructions for a small imploding bomb. It showed the correct positions of the electronic detonator and the placement of five small vials.

Chuck struggled with the questions the diagram raised. "A bomb? This small?" he whispered. "Why?"

The window rattled and the wind tore a shutter loose from its latching.

Hours later, when the house was quiet, Chuck picked up the telephone. A strange clicking in the instrument gave him alarm and he hung up without making his call. He found his jacket and the keys to the truck and left the house through the back door. He was only three steps away from the house when he was stopped. A man in a rain poncho, carrying a high-powered automatic weapon stepped out of the dark.

"No!" the man barked. "You go back!"

"But I need to go to town. I have—I have business," Chuck argued.

The man raised the gun to point at Chuck's chest. The message was clear.

Chapter 9

Chuck paced the darkened house while the storm buffeted the walls seeking means of entry. Around two A.M. he tried the telephone and found that the line was dead. Finally, he climbed the dining room stairs, walked past the guards stationed outside Ahmed's and Omar's bedrooms and climbed the narrow stairs to Joey's attic bedroom.

Joey had stayed at the house after delivering the package to Ahmed and now was on his bed with the one window wide open despite the rain.

Chuck shook the boy awake. "I've got to try to get to town," he whispered. "I'm betting Randolph and Martin are still close by."

Joey rubbed his eyes. "Why? What's up?"

Chuck showed him the paper. "There was a letter with the last package. Beth found it. I'm afraid to think what we have in this house. Omar's guards aren't letting anybody out."

"What do you want me to do?" Joey asked, alert now.

"Go to the stable, tell them you need to check the horses, anything, just keep them busy for a few minutes. I'm going to go out on the roof to the oak. If I can get out of the yard, I'll be okay."

"What happens if you don't make it?" Joey asked.

Chuck was silent, then spoke carefully. "Then I want you to . . . " his hand shook as he clasped Joey's knee. "I want you to get out, get Beth out and call the sheriff's department. Tell them these men are constructing some kind of bomb here in the house. They'll take it from there."

Joey quickly got dressed.

"Go now," the young pastor urged him. "And be convincing."

Joey tromped downstairs without trying to hide his movement. He took his rain jacket off the peg by the back door, found the flashlight in the cupboard and went outside.

He whistled, half to control the fear in his stomach and half to alert the men outside to the innocence of his intentions. His flashlight beam cut a wavery path in the dark and the rain looked like silver pellets falling through the narrow shaft of light.

He didn't even make it to the cars parked behind the house before a cloaked figure stepped into his path.

"Go back," the voice ordered.

Joey shone his light in the man's face and the reaction was instantaneous. The man jumped out of the light and aimed his rifle at the boy.

"Hey, I'm just going to the stable. See?" He shone the light toward the structure one hundred yards distance. Fortunately, one of the horses was uneasy and neighed.

"The storm's made the horses jumpy. I'm just going to check on them."

The man looked Joey over carefully then grudgingly waved him on. He stayed close behind him and watched as Joey entered each stall. Joey felt he had used as much time as he dared, when he heard a rattle of automatic gunfire outside.

He ran out of the stable, pushing the guard aside. Men were calling to one another in the night but Joey understood nothing they said. He ran for the front of the house.

"Stop! Stop!" the man behind him cried. A burst of gunfire and the thud, thud, thud of bullets at his feet froze Joey in his tracks. The guard reached him and grabbed his arm. He could see two men running toward the front of the house toward the giant oak that brushed the roof. A crumpled figure lay at the base of the tree.

"Chuck!" Joey screamed.

The guard left Joey and ran to join his partner. Joey's first impulse was to force his way to the fallen man. But he remembered Chuck's instructions and how hard it had been for Chuck to give them.

Joey gave a wrenching cry and ran for the house. Beth and Ahmed were in the parlor staring at the activity and trying to figure out what had happened. Omar, in a flowing silk robe, looking irritated by the interruption to his sleep, strode through the room and went outside.

"You murderer!" Joey screamed at Ahmed as he grabbed Beth's arm and pulled her away from the window.

"Who is it?" Ahmed asked. "They shot somebody?"

"They shot Chuck!" Joey cried. "You and your lousy guards shot Chuck!"

Ahmed shook his head. "There's been some mistake, a terrible mistake."

Beth screamed and tried to pull away.

"There's been a mistake all right!" Joey shouted, holding Beth's wrist tightly. "Trusting you! There was a letter with that last package, but I don't suppose you know anything about that, or about a bomb!" He pulled Beth toward the back of the house. She was sobbing and struggling.

Joey shook her hard. "We've got to get out of here!" he yelled at her. "Be hysterical later! These people are killers!"

"No!" Ahmed cried as he followed them. "No! There is only gold, gold for a purchase of rifles, not a bomb!"

"There's no gold!" Joey spat at him. "I opened one." He pulled Beth out the back door. "You're either the best liar I ever met, Mr. Crown Prince, or else you're the biggest fool."

Propelling Beth ahead of him, Joey headed for the stables. He bridled the horses and forced Beth to mount Nutmeg bareback. They went straight for the woods. Within minutes they were soaked from the rain. Beth, looking like a wet rag doll in her nightie, cried until only an occasional whimper was left. Joey took her to his bower, forced her through the thicket and pulled dry clothes from his cache.

"Put these on," he ordered. "I'm going for help. And stay here. You can wrap that tarp around you. Furball's around here somewhere. He'll guard you."

He knelt down to crawl out of the leafy enclosure. "Just don't go back to the house, whatever you do. Understand? I don't want to lose you, too."

Beth gulped and nodded, clutching the dry clothes to her chest. When he was gone, the night closed in. The storm thrashed the tops of the trees and made howling sounds in the upper branches. But the storm could not come below where Beth sat. Furball whined and crawled through the opening. He sniffed Beth carefully then lay down at her feet.

Once she was changed and dry, she unfolded the tarp and wrapped it around herself like a cocoon. Lying on the soft bed of leaves and pine needles, she was quiet until the grief inside welled up and broke out again in tears.

"It's such an ugly world, God," she sobbed. "Why don't you do something? It's such an ugly, ugly world."

―――――――――

Joey's words had hit Ahmed like a blow. The implications of what he'd said were more than he could accept. He ran to the front yard to Chuck's side. The young pastor had been hit twice, once in the leg and once in the shoulder. He was alive but bleeding badly.

"Get help!" Ahmed shouted. "Call a doctor!"

Omar yanked at his shoulder. "Where are the other two?" he demanded.

Ahmed pressed his hands against the wound in Chuck's shoulder to slow the bleeding. The man moaned.

"I told you to get this man some help!" Ahmed roared. "Have I ceased to give orders around here?"

Omar sent two of the guards away. "Search the house!" he directed them. "One of you should have stayed at your post. I told you no one was to leave this house alive."

Ahmed stood up and faced the professor. There was blood on the young man's hands. "Who are you?" Ahmed seethed. "You are no emissary from my father! You order *my* bodyguards to shoot innocent people and now you leave this man to bleed to death? Why are you doing this?"

Omar pushed Ahmed to the ground. "You are not the issue here. You pompous little fool! Jorge always said you were too naive to rule and he was right!"

Omar gave the other two guards directions and the men disappeared into the storm. Then Omar strode into the house. Ahmed ran after him.

"You are an imbecile!" Omar stormed. "Do you want to jeopardize everything we've planned and worked for for years in order to help that American? Don't you know what these Americans have done to us? Look at our country, we're just pawns, pawns for America to use. *Use*, Ahmed. We're tired of being used. And your precious father would sell us out again, in a minute. We go to the base tomorrow, as planned," Omar told him. "Nothing will stop us, nothing, do you understand? Not that man out there and not you either!"

"To deliver gold? You do all this to deliver some gold?"

"We are not taking gold," Omar admitted. "We're *destroying* gold."

Ahmed stood very still. "Destroying . . . ? Does my father . . . ? Did Father order this?"

Omar sneered at the bewildered young man. "Am I not closest to your father?"

Ahmed was still standing in the parlor when Omar returned downstairs dressed to go outside.

"My father's friend?" he whispered as he watched Omar leave. "No," he breathed. "You have never been my father's friend."

He looked around the room as though searching for an answer, some way of escape, then, realizing what he had to do, he climbed the parlor stairs.

Joey rode hard through the woods, using deer paths only he and the wild animals knew. When he reached the lake road he kicked King hard and galloped for town. Even at a dead run, he knew he was no match for the car that would, in time, catch up with him.

Joey was chilled by the wind and rain hitting against his face. King was lathered and strained to keep up the grueling pace. As soon as he entered Cooper's Creek, Joey headed for Gus Tuten's garage and the pay telephone under the tree beside the gas pumps. He fumbled in his pockets for change and groaned when he found none. For a moment he didn't know what to do. Then he found a stick and broke out one of the windows in the garage. Once inside, he found the telephone and called the emergency number.

"Old Post Road," he stammered. "A man's been shot and—and you'd better call the CIA, if you have their number. Tell Mr. Randolph to come back. Tell him there's a bomb in the house."

He answered the few questions the dispatcher had, then slowly hung up the phone. Convulsive sobs shook him and only when he saw King standing patiently in the rain, did he pull himself together.

He found some rags, left a note of apology for Gus and a promise to pay for the damages and let himself out the door. He cried in the rain as he rubbed King down, then remounted slowly and left the sleeping town.

An hour later he was back at the copse in the woods. He tied King beside Nutmeg and found Beth fast asleep under the tarp. He managed to start a small fire with the leaves and kindling he kept hidden in the hollow tree. Once the fire caught, he sat cross-legged in front of it and waited, prayed, for morning.

———————————

Randolph and Martin were in Coeur d'Alene with Chief Harrison when the call came through. "It's broken open," Harrison said when he slammed down the receiver. "Come on. It's not what we thought."

The men raced to their car and radioed for additional help. "We should've pulled those people out of there," Randolph said when he heard about Chuck. "He must have stumbled onto something."

They drove through every stop light and raced at high speeds to the boarding house. Had Martin been less expert a driver they would have slid off the road on any one of several mud-slickened curves. As they pulled into the driveway, they heard shots coming from the woods. Martin screeched the car to a stop on the south side of the house, jumped from the car, guns in hand and crawled to where Chuck lay. An ambulance careened down the road and the driver, hearing the gunfire, passed the boarding house without stopping. Martin pulled Chuck to their car. Harrison used their radio to communicate with the ambulance. "Come up from the south," he directed them "and bring a stretcher. This man is bleeding badly." Then he called for backup help. Randolph kept up return fire as the paramedics crawled in and took Chuck away.

The exchange of bullets was sporadic as each side attempted to keep the other from moving. Down the lane, when he heard the firing at the house, Omar abandoned his pursuit of Beth and Joey and returned with one of his men. He commanded the other man to find the escapees or not to bother to return at all.

By the time Omar reached the boarding house, Martin's backup units had arrived, and the firing in the trees north of the house was now aimed in the opposite direction. With the men in the trees pinned down, Martin dashed for the house. He saw Omar and his man in the dining room and didn't wait to ask questions. He saw the guard prepare to shoot and opened fire himself, wounding the guard.

"We have diplomatic immunity!" Omar screamed, holding up his hands.

Martin ran to take the gun from the guard. "We'll see how kindly our government takes to your style of diplomacy."

Randolph came inside. "They've rounded up the men in the woods. There were only two of them." He kept his gun aimed at Omar and helped Martin herd their charges up the dining room stairs.

"We'll see how peaceful this mission of yours really is," Martin said. "Then we'll talk about diplomatic immunity."

———————

In the woods, the lone hunter kept on the lane, scanning the trees, realizing the longer he looked, how difficult his job was. An hour later, he saw the horses. He carefully pushed his way through the undergrowth and three hundred feet into the woods, saw the flicker of Joey's campfire.

He shifted the safety off his gun and crept closer.

Furball heard him coming seconds before Joey did. The wolf-dog raised up on his haunches and growled. Joey tried to douse the fire with dirt and realized he didn't have time. He scrambled up the huge oak at his back. Beth slept peacefully on.

The man crashed through the bushes guarding the copse. He saw the sleeping girl and the wolf-dog at the same instant.

Beth rolled over, wakened by the noise. "Joey?" she called sleepily. Furball tensed to spring.

The man saw the wild animal and aimed to fire.

"No!" Joey screamed from his perch in the tree, and then he jumped. He landed on the man's back, throwing the shot wild. Furball sprang and Beth woke up, wondering if she was having a bad dream.

"Get his gun! Get his gun!" Joey yelled as the three bodies rolled in the bushes.

Beth groped around the twisting mess of legs and arms until she found the pistol. She held it in both hands and shakily aimed it at the group on the ground.

"Freeze!" she yelled.

The man ignored her and continued struggling to fend off Furball's teeth and club Joey away.

Beth moved her aim to the side and pulled the trigger. The kick from the gun wrenched her arm and threw her off balance. But the shot convinced the guard to lie still. Furball stood on his chest, fangs bared in the man's face. Joey scrambled free. He found some cord in his stash and tied the man's hands together. Then he pulled them over the man's head and secured them to a tree. He took another length of cord and did the same to the man's feet so that the guard's body was stretched out like a hammock. Then Joey took the pistol out of Beth's hands.

"You're dangerous!" he said once he had it.

Beth just nodded and clasped her hands together to keep them from shaking.

"I think we'd better go to the house," Joey decided. "We're not safe here. Besides, the sheriff's officers ought to be there by now."

"What about him?" Beth asked, pointing.

"Furball will take care of him," Joey replied. "Won't you boy?" He stroked the dog's head and the animal moved off the man's body and lay facing him.

Joey stomped out the fire. In the dark, only Furball's one eye and white fangs showed. Each time the man made the slightest move, the animal pulled back his lips and snarled. The man didn't take his eyes off the animal and tried very hard not to move a muscle.

———————————

Dr. Neiber came out of hiding in his room when he heard the shooting outside stop. When Martin and Randolph came upstairs with Omar and the wounded guard, they saw the wizened old man standing in the hall.

Omar had regained his composure. "This is a serious matter. My men were only acting in defense of Ahmed. As you well know, there has already been an attempt on his life."

"You want us to believe Chuck Warren was a threat to Ahmed?" Randolph asked. He pushed Omar into the bedroom he'd been occupying and went directly to the black steamer trunk.

"Mr. Warren was shot while trying to leave the house," Martin said. "That's pretty obvious."

Omar's hesitation was hardly perceptible. He watched as Randolph opened the trunk. "He was trying to undermine the entire purpose of our trip. He was a threat to my country's security and had to be stopped. He was warned."

Dr. Neiber stood at the open door and said nothing.

"See this," Randolph motioned to his partner. Martin let the wounded guard slump to the floor and kept his gun aimed at the two prisoners as he moved to see what was inside the trunk.

Randolph broke open the ebony base.

"There is no law, international or otherwise forbidding the movement of gold!" Omar stated hurriedly.

"Gold bullion?" Randolph asked. He pulled one of the small oblong wooden boxes out of the interior of the ebony base. It's lid was broken and he easily opened it.

Martin took his eyes off Omar long enough to

look. It was a moment too long.

Omar leapt for the dresser and grabbed a small silver disc lying on it. Martin swung around and prepared to shoot.

"Don't!" Omar snarled. "Or you'll die."

"We'll all die, Professor," Dr. Neiber assured him quietly. "But I don't care. I am dead already." The CIA agents looked curiously at the strange little man.

"What do you mean?" Martin asked, still holding his gun aimed at Omar.

"He means that if I move my hand, a small device inside that silver globe in the trunk will cause it to implode," Omar explained. "Not a large implosion, but adequate to release the contents of the globe."

"And that, gentlemen, would be lethal," Neiber added. "It is plutonium 200, highly radioactive. If the dust scatters, it contaminates everything it touches, for longer than a lifetime. This entire house would have to be destroyed. Even the land would be useless."

Martin lowered his gun.

"The army base," Randolph pieced together. "There's gold there. That's it, isn't it? You're going to contaminate the gold."

Omar smiled.

The wounded guard moaned and fell over on the floor. Omar glanced at him and Randolph took advantage of that brief interruption to throw the brick at the professor.

It struck Omar's arm, but not before he pushed the button.

Chapter 10

Nothing happened. Omar gasped, grabbed the detonator and pressed it again.

Martin raised his gun. No one moved. Then Dr. Neiber walked to the trunk and lifted the heavy silver globe out. He set it on the floor.

"Don't open it!" Omar screamed. "We'll be irradiated!"

Neiber looked at Randolph. "It may be true. Perhaps you should leave the house. I assembled it one afternoon when no one was here. The radiation itself is deadly. It is like a laser beam; it goes through whatever is in its way although it contaminates nothing. Non-life forms are not affected."

"But you . . . "

"I am a dead man."

"Why?" Randolph asked. "Why would you, would anyone do . . . ?"

"My wife is in Shamir. We are a religious minority there. She was arrested for taking part in a coup. Of course, the coup was orchestrated by the good professor here."

Omar glared at the little scientist.

Neiber continued speaking: "When I secured the detonation device, I did make one way it could be defused."

Martin and Randolph waited.

"If the globe was opened, the detonator would become inoperable. But, of course whoever opened it would die." Dr. Neiber hesitated. "I warned him it would kill him," he murmured.

"That wasn't in my plans!" Omar fumed.

"It was the only safety device I could manage without more sophisticated tools," the little man explained sadly.

"We'll leave the house," Randolph decided. "Then open the globe."

He and Martin escorted Omar and the guard outside. They found the other lawmen in the front yard with prisoners in tow. Randolph explained the situation and moved everyone out to the road.

Minutes ticked by. Dr. Neiber came to the front porch. Even in the porch light, his face looked pale. "It is gone!" he yelled. "The container with the vials is gone! He has taken it!" And Dr. Neiber knew in that moment what had happened.

After the confrontation with Joey, Ahmed had walked upstairs. Down the hall, a door opened and Dr. Neiber had peeked out to see whose footsteps he had heard. Ahmed was deep inside himself and did not see.

Neiber was surprised to see the young prince enter not his own room, but Omar's. Ahmed was standing in front of the trunk when the doctor joined him there.

"Come to gloat over your handiwork?" the old man had asked in the desert tongue.

Ahmed looked around sharply, seeing the man for the first time. "I do not know what this is," he said.

Dr. Neiber did not try to mask his disgust. He looked at the young man and, making a decision, spoke his mind. "You have left a trail of dead bodies behind you, including mine, and you pretend to me that you don't know what you've done?" His laugh was full of scorn.

Dr. Neiber remembered the sudden physical weakness that had overcome him then and how he had sat down in one of the chairs near the window. He removed his glasses and wiped them in an automatic gesture as he stared at the confusion in Ahmed's face. "You are a convincing actor," he stated. "You will do well in politics, although I do not see the purpose of it here, now."

"There is gold bullion here," Ahmed declared hopefully. "Omar just told me. The arms deal . . . "

Neiber snorted. "You can do better than that. Look outside. Would these men kill over such a small horde as this?"

Then Ahmed opened the trunk. The silver globe shone like a mirror, catching all light and throwing it back. "But what, then?" he paused and looked at the aging scientist. "Why are you here?"

Dr. Neiber stared at him. "You don't know," he realized. "You really don't know, do you?"

Ahmed strained to lift the heavy globe out of

the trunk. It weighed nearly eighty pounds. He set it on the bed, then unsuccessfully attempted to lift out the ebony base.

"What are you doing?" Neiber demanded.

Ahmed would not answer. He opened the ebony base where it lay in the trunk, pulled out one of the five wooden boxes inside, and pried open the lid.

"Not gold," he said when he was the lead brick. "None of them."

Neiber shook his head. "Of course not."

"My father did not send gold to buy arms." Ahmed did not know whether to be relieved or terrified.

Neiber's face relaxed. "Your father didn't send anything. This is the professor's doing. But the world will never know that. When this poison destroys that base tomorrow . . . "

"The base? John Trevor is stationed at that base. What is in here?" he asked, gliding his hand over the globe, tripping the latch.

"Don't touch it!" Neiber warned, "It cost me my life to assemble it. What is inside will eat you up like a massive dose of x-rays. I am expendable to men like Professor Omar, but not you. No."

Then the little man walked to the bedroom door. "I could open it, I suppose. I can only die once. But you see, there is someone I love who would die too, far away and all alone. Right now I would watch the whole world destroy itself if only to save her. But how can you understand such love? You and your father live in a different world. It is your problem now, not mine." Then the scientist left the room. As he stood on the porch and called out his news to Martin, he could only imagine the rest of what Ahmed had done.

Beth and Joey, on horseback, were in sight of the house when a car pulled away from the parking area and turned down the lane. Martin was driving and when he pulled alongside the riders, he rolled down his window and asked, "Have you seen Ahmed?"

Omar was sitting in the back seat with Randolph, and Dr. Neiber sat in the front seat between Martin and Chief Harrison.

"No, why?" Joey asked. "What about Chuck?"

"He's out of danger," Martin said. "Where would Ahmed go if he wanted to dump something, get rid of say, a small heavy package?"

Joey looked puzzled.

"The quarry!" Beth guessed. "I bet he'd take it to the quarry, to the old mine shaft!"

"Why there?"

"Where else?" Beth shrugged. "I told him how it would be a perfect dump site, it's so deep. It's just a hassle to get there."

Joey reined King around and kicked the horse into a gallop.

"We'll follow," Martin shouted as he shifted the car into gear.

Beth stayed close to the car. Their speed was slower than Joey's because the lane was deeply rutted from years of rain and runoff.

Joey pushed King as hard as he dared in the dark. He had a terrible feeling they would be too late.

Ahmed had stood staring at the globe for a long time before reaching out to open the tiny clasp. Knowing full well what he was doing, he opened the lid. Inside the thick lead casing that made the globe so heavy was a small metal cup containing five glass vials. In the center of the cup was an intricately assembled container with electrical wires running out to the shell of the globe.

Ahmed pulled the wires off the explosive device and lifted the cup free from its protective nest. Although he felt nothing, and in spite of the fact that the plutonium was sealed inside the vials, he knew the killing rays were already being absorbed into his flesh and bones.

He set the small cup on the bed, closed the globe and returned it to the trunk. When he was done, the room looked exactly as he had found it. He picked up the deadly cup, and clutching it to his chest, stumbled downstairs and out of the house.

He heard the gunfire in the front yard, but paid no attention to it. He set his face toward the quarry and began his long walk.

Forty-five minutes later he was on the quarry path. He went straight to the mine and, ignoring the warning signs, walked into the dark tunnel, looking for the shaft where the poison could plummet to a depth where it could harm no one again.

Joey found Ahmed there, at the edge of the shaft, lying in the dark on the cold, hard earth. Chief Harrison was behind the boy and shone the flashlight on the still figure at their feet.

"Ahmed?" Joey whispered. "Are you okay?"

"Let's get him out of here," Harrison said. "This place is like a tomb." They lifted Ahmed up and carried him outside.

Dawn was only minutes away when they laid

Ahmed on the grass. The sky was turning pink in the east, routing the darkness.

"It's over," Ahmed whispered. "They wanted me to believe this was my father's plan, but it was a lie. I knew it was a lie!" Tears rolled off his face.

Beth led Randolph through the trees. She hesitated to come near. "Dr. Neiber says you shouldn't have held it. That stuff is really radioactive."

"I could not carry it so far any other way," Ahmed explained. "It was too heavy."

Beth met Ahmed's eyes and seeing the quiet acceptance of the price he'd paid, she burst into tears. He held out his arms to her and she unashamedly ran into his embrace.

Ahmed looked at Joey over Beth's head and held out his hand to him. Joey took it and held the hand clasp.

Harrison and Randolph left them there. They did not see dawn come.

Sheriff Paul Larsen and his wife arrived home on the following Friday. Chuck had been returned from the hospital that morning and was lying on the couch in the living room, his arm in a sling, and a big bandage around his shoulder and chest.

"Looks like you had a boring few weeks," the sheriff said, noting the bullet holes in the wall of the dining room. "I stopped in at the office and got the whole report."

Virginia hugged her daughter and saw a new deepness in her eyes. "You're not the same, are you, Button?"

Beth looked away. "No," she replied slowly.

Chuck called everyone into the living room to watch the evening news on television. They waited until the announcer's voice droned out the circus of world events.

Paul sat beside Virginia on the couch. "Did that young man really know what exposing himself to the plutonium would mean?"

Chuck nodded. "Dr. Neiber swears he made it very clear to Ahmed that the radiation alone would kill him."

"Yet he knowingly exposed himself?" Virginia mused.

"I think he made a very careful decision," Chuck explained.

Beth moved to sit at her mother's feet and listened.

"He was always aware that he represented his father," Chuck continued.

Joey pulled his gaze from the television and nodded. "Yeah, he kept talking about his dad. 'My father would do this. My father wants that.'"

Chuck searched Joey's and Beth's faces to see if either one of them really understood.

"Ahmed represented his father in much the same way as Jesus Christ represented His Father. When Ahmed saw that his father's purposes had been sabotaged, that his character was being unjustly profaned, he did what he had to do to rectify it."

Joey stared unseeingly at the television. "That walk down the quarry path was his walk to Golgotha, wasn't it?"

The question went unanswered as the picture on the screen changed to Los Angeles International Airport. The announcer continued his nightly newscast.

"The crown prince of Shamir wrapped up a successful tour of the United States this weekend," he said over camera shots of Ahmed and a group of body guards walking to a waiting jet. Ahmed wore one of his tailored suits.

"The cultural tour was cut short by several days because of the prince's deteriorating health, but all reports admit that the young man's visit was a huge step in verifying his father's peaceful overtures to this country. Emissaries are now in Washington, charting out an unprecedented trade agreement between the two nations."

Ahmed walked slowly toward the steps to board the jet. Halfway there, he faltered and had to be assisted. As he turned to face the cameras, a reporter pushed a microphone in his face.

"You received quite a few gifts while you were here," the reporter stated. "Which was the most valuable?"

Ahmed lowered his head. "Many lovely gifts are returning with me to Shamir," he said, his voice weak. "But this," he reached inside his coat pocket, "this one is the most cherished." He pulled out his baseball cap.

"What a price he paid!" Virginia whispered.

Beth was unaware of the tears running down her cheeks.

Ahmed, at that moment, put the cap on his head, looked directly into the camera, smiled, and waved good-bye.

The door to the side porch was open. Beth, with tear-blurred vision, stared through the screen at the sun filtering through the new leaf buds on the trees.

Winter was over.